An Unexpected

A *Twickenham* **Time Travel Romance**

By:

Laura Beers

Chapter 1

May 2018

Clutching the keys to her family's historic Boston brownstone in her hand, Amelia Wright hastily unlocked her door and pushed it open.

"Goodnight, Brian." She tossed the words over her shoulder, attempting to close the door as quickly as possible.

Her tall, lanky date put his hand out and stopped the door, apparently not taking the hint. As he leaned against the jamb, he grinned suggestively, revealing something stuck between his top front teeth.

"Aren't you going to invite me in?" he prompted, his tongue wetting his chapped bottom lip.

She reluctantly turned back towards him and debated jabbing him in the throat with her keys, thus ending the night on a high note. Instead, sanity prevailed, and she offered him a tight smile.

"No, I don't think that would be the best idea."

His blue eyes perused her face, making her decidedly uncomfortable. "This may be our first official date, but we both can feel the chemistry between us." He stepped closer to her, his black Birkenstocks crossing the threshold of the door. "All the residents at the hospital told me not to waste my time since you're married to your work." His eyes darted towards her lips. "However, I find your aloofness incredibly… sexy."

"I see." Amelia folded her arms across her burgundy cashmere sweater. "Tell me, do the other residents think I'm 'aloof' as well?"

"They sure do," Brian blundered on. "But they're just jealous because you're the top obstetrics resident." Unbelievably, he started to lean in towards her.

Was that supposed to pass for a compliment? Amelia shook her head as she put up her hand to stop him from advancing further. "Goodnight." Her tone left no room for argument.

He threw his hands in the air and protested, "I bought you dinner tonight!"

Reaching into the depths of her black Prada handbag, she pulled out a twenty-dollar bill and held it out to him. "Keep the change."

After an awkward pause, Brian grabbed the money and shoved it into the pocket of his green cargo shorts. "You are just like the other residents said. I don't know why I bothered."

Feeling the heat rising in her cheeks, Amelia's reply dripped with sarcasm. "*Did* you bother? After all, I thoroughly enjoyed our *romantic* dinner at Taco Bell."

He frowned. "I guess I'll see you around the hospital." Shaking his head, he turned and stomped towards the black, iron fence that lined the shallow front yard of her brownstone. He slammed the gate shut, the angry reverberations echoing through the quiet street.

Good heavens, that was awkward, Amelia thought. Closing the door, she latched the bolt and tossed her keys onto the side table in the receiving foyer. She kicked off her

Louboutin heels as she heaved a sigh. Walking barefoot across the polished hardwood floor, she took the hair tie from around her wrist and placed her thick, wavy, brown hair into a ponytail.

Climbing the narrow staircase, her steps faltered as she saw her reflection in the Palladian window. She may have inherited her father's piercing green eyes, but she was the spitting image of her mother with high cheekbones, full lips, and a fair complexion. Over the years, many men had vied for her attention, but she wasn't interested. Her focus had always been excelling in medical school and becoming the best doctor she could be. Above all, she wanted to make her parents proud.

She walked up the last few steps, reached the parlor level, and headed towards the living room, hoping to speak to her mother before she went to bed.

The housekeeper, Mrs. Lopez, emerged from the kitchen and greeted her. "How are you, Miss Amelia?"

"I am well, now that I'm home, thank you." Amelia smiled at the aged housekeeper. "Is my mother still awake?"

"She is. I was just about to get Mrs. Lottie her bedtime snack," Mrs. Lopez said, waving back towards the kitchen.

Amelia followed her and watched as the housekeeper reached into the freezer, pulled out a carton of ice cream and dished it into two bowls.

Opening a drawer, Amelia grabbed two spoons and placed them into the bowls. "Is Dustin gone for the evening?"

"You mean Lord Wessex?"

She huffed in amusement. "I have no idea why my mother refers to Dustin as 'Lord Wessex'."

"He left after dinner." Mrs. Lopez extended a bowl towards Amelia. "I do not think I have seen a more dedicated nurse than him."

Amelia nodded. "I agree. He's been a blessing to Mom. You both have."

Picking up the other bowl, Mrs. Lopez laughed as she started towards the south-facing living room with a floor-to-ceiling, stone fireplace. "You best not let Mrs. Lottie hear you call her '*Mom*'."

She laughed. "I know. She prefers it when I call her '*Mum*'."

Her mother's voice spoke up from the white couch. "Of course, I do. After all, you are half British, my dear."

"And, according to Father, I am half civilized," Amelia teased.

"It's true," the aging Lottie Wright agreed from her perch on the leather couch. She accepted the bowl of ice cream and thanked her housekeeper with old-world graciousness. Then she turned her attention to her daughter. "How was your date?"

Amelia plopped down on an overstuffed white leather chair as Mrs. Lopez slipped out of the room. "It was horrible." She spooned a bite of chocolate heaven into her mouth and let it melt before continuing, "I don't know why I let you talk me into going on a date with Brian Hostetter."

"Because Brian's mother was one of my dearest friends during my days at university," her mother explained, pointing her spoon at Amelia. "I do hope you were nice to him."

Amelia paused, her spoon hovering above the bowl. She prodded cautiously, "And do you remember where you attended university, Mum?"

Placing a hand to her forehead, her mother's expression became confused. "I don't remember."

"You went to Oxford," she reminded her gently.

"Yes, I remember now," her mother exclaimed proudly. "And Brian's mother was named Olivia. We were flatmates."

Tapping the spoon against her lips, Amelia jested, "I think it is time for you to make new friends."

"Oh, dear. The date was that bad?"

"I don't know why I bothered," she muttered, scooping up the last bite. "Gentlemen don't exist anymore."

Her mother gave her a wry look. "How would you know? This was your first date since you started Harvard Medical School, and that was almost seven years ago."

"I don't have *time* to date, Mum," Amelia explained for the thousandth time. "Besides, I won't settle for anything less than what you and Father had."

"Perhaps you will fall madly in love with an English gentleman on our holiday," her mother teased as she placed the empty bowl on the stand beside her. "After all, I fell in love with an American on one of my journeys abroad."

Frowning, Amelia eyed her mother's withered frame, but it was the dimming light in her once-bright eyes that frightened her most of all. Charlotte Wright was in the moderate stages of Alzheimer's, but she had other health troubles as well. Happily, her mother was lucid right now, but there were times that she seemed to forget her own name. "I still think this vacation is a bad idea."

"Pish-posh," her mother dismissed Amelia's concerns with a wave. "I must say goodbye to my dear friend, Aunt Nellie."

"You could just call her and save all the hassle of flying to England," Amelia, ever the practical daughter, attempted again.

"We must go back to Twickenham Manor for the monthly Full Moon Ball," her mother insisted, then lowered her voice to a mere whisper. "That is where the *magic* is."

"Yes, Mum," Amelia sighed, knowing this was a losing battle. "But I'll be monitoring your vitals constantly."

Her mother smiled fondly at her. "It's a good thing I am traveling with my talented doctor daughter."

Amelia rose and returned her smile. "May I help you back to your room?"

Her mother shook her head. "No, I wish to stay up a little longer."

"Don't stay up too late," Amelia warned. "We are catching an early flight to London tomorrow."

"I remember."

She went and kissed her mother's wrinkly cheek before heading to her bedroom upstairs. After changing into her pajamas, she curled up on the tufted seat of her bay window, staring out over Boston's night skyline.

Amelia's heart constricted at the reminder that her mother's time on this earth was coming to an end. Her parents, Devon and Charlotte Wright, had married later in life, and their only daughter wasn't born until they were in their mid-40's. Not that she was complaining, because she'd had a perfect childhood. Her parents had always been attentive, loving, and kind. Her thoughts stilled, and her lower lip quivered as she remembered her father.

He had been one of the top orthopedic surgeons in Boston when the accident had cut his life short. Her father had been called in for an emergency surgery and was traveling to the hospital when a driver ran through a red light, causing his car to flip. He'd died on the scene. Suddenly, the life that Lottie and Amelia had known was over.

Now, only a few years later, her mother had been diagnosed with congestive heart failure, but Amelia suspected she was dying more from a broken heart. She leaned her head against the cool window pane and sighed. When her mother passed, Amelia would be left alone in this vast, highly-desirable brownstone in Boston. In the current real estate market, as Amelia was aware, the house would fetch at least ten million dollars. But the thought of such a staggering sum meant nothing to Amelia. No amount of money would ever replace her mother. She blinked back the tears forming in her eyes.

Reaching under a pillow, she removed her well-worn copy of *Pride and Prejudice*. It was a first edition copy, signed by Jane Austen herself. No matter what she chose to do with the house, Amelia knew that she would never part with this priceless family heirloom. It was, ironically, inscribed to another woman nicknamed Lottie.

Slowly, Amelia ran her fingers over the green morocco label and gilt tooling on the cover before she opened the book and traced her mother's name in black ink. Her mother used to share stories of how she was friends with Jane and even claimed that she helped brainstorm the book idea of *Emma* with her. She smiled, knowing her mother always had a vivid imagination.

Tucking her feet under herself on the window seat, she clutched the book to her chest, gazing at the lights of Boston's Longwood Medical Area. For the past seven years, she had practically lived at that facility, going through the grueling demands of Harvard Medical School. Now, she was a third-year resident in obstetrics.

Amelia should have been excited by the prospect of her future, but instead, her heart ached at the gnawing loneliness she felt daily. Since her father was gone, and her own mother sometimes failed to recognize her, she felt… lost.

The next day, the black cab rolled up to the main entrance of Twickenham Manor, and Amelia felt the smile on her face grow at the flood of happy memories surrounding this estate. From an early age, her family would travel to London to participate in the Regency Immersion package offered here. Although these kinds of packages hadn't been commonly offered elsewhere for very long, Twickenham Manor had been offering them for more than a hundred years.

Exiting the cab, Amelia put up her hand to shade her eyes, admiring the massive towers and battlements of the four-story, pristinely white mansion that was almost a castle. She hopped over to her mother's side and opened the cab door as the driver unloaded their luggage from the hatchback.

After tipping the cab driver, Amelia started wheeling the two large suitcases towards the main door while her mother kept her gaze firmly on the Manor. "Every time I see this place, it is no less impressive," her mother stated. She wore the wistful smile of one who has returned home after a long absence.

As they sauntered into the main foyer, Amelia could not help but be intrigued by the ornate woodwork, bold, red-papered walls and elaborate gold ceilings. Red velvet settees sat in alcoves, and a Turkish rug the size of a skating rink ran the length of the hall. "This entire estate looks as if it was plucked out of the 1800s," Amelia expressed as she admired the window coverings.

"Lottie Wright!" Aunt Nellie exclaimed as she bustled into the foyer from a side door.

As Amelia watched the beautiful lady cross the room to greet her mother, she smiled. She had always called her "Aunt Nellie," even though she knew they weren't related. Cocking her head, she attempted to pinpoint her exact age, but Nellie could have been thirty or sixty, for all she knew. She appeared ageless. Her face held no wrinkles, but her eyes spoke of extreme wisdom and wit. She dressed in classic, timeless clothing and wore her hair in simple, short waves that framed her face perfectly. Not a hint of the infirmities of age slowed her graceful steps, although Amelia knew she must be older than she appeared. Aunt Nellie stepped back from embracing her mother and turned her gaze towards her.

"Amelia." She smiled that same bright smile that seemed to light up any room.

Leaving the luggage, she went and embraced Nellie. Even though they were not related, this lady held a special place in her heart. "Aunt Nellie, it is so good to see you! I did not think it was possible, but you seem younger than when I last saw you over seven years ago."

"It must be because of my good doctors." Aunt Nellie winked, her bright blue eyes snapping with mischief. "Now, my darlings, I have set you both up in your usual rooms. They are fully stocked with gowns, slippers, fans, and everything you need for the Regency Immersion Experience."

Removing the cellphone from her back pocket, Amelia tucked it into her purse while saying, "Please say that I will not be required to attend the classes or read any of the manuals that ensure I have a full understanding of the Regency times and customs."

Aunt Nellie gave her an understanding smile. "Considering you came every summer faithfully until you started Harvard, I think you can forego the training."

"Thank you," Amelia replied. "And do I really need to wear a corset?"

"Don't push it, young lady," Aunt Nellie admonished, winking again to let her know that she was teasing. "I know you both must be famished, but the Full Moon Ball is in a few hours. Why don't you head up to your rooms and rest until it is time to dress for dinner?"

"Do you suppose any old friends will be popping in for a visit while we're here?" Lottie asked, her rheumy eyes roaming the portraits on the wall.

Aunt Nellie reached over and placed her arm around Lottie's shoulders. "One could only hope, but let's get you to your room, shall we?"

Keeping her pace respectfully slow behind them, Amelia heard her mother say, "I don't think my body could handle time travel anymore, Nellie."

"I believe you may be right, dear," Aunt Nellie murmured, patting her friend's shoulder as the trio made their way down the galleried hall.

Amelia stifled a sigh, knowing that her mother wasn't mentally there. She hoped a rest would break her out of her fantasy. Suddenly, Lottie stopped the procession and turned her head to look for her daughter. "I do hope for your sake that Lord Harrington will be here tonight."

"Who is Lord Harrington, Mum?" she asked, utterly bewildered.

A girlish smile came to Lottie's lips, and her eyes sparkled. "Ooh, he is a handsome earl, whose lands border Twickenham Manor to the east."

Amelia tried to recall a time when her mother had talked about a Lord Harrington, but she couldn't think of one. "Did you meet him when you were studying at Oxford, perhaps?" she asked, prodding her mother's memory. Nellie wordlessly guided her longtime friend further along the hall as mother and daughter continued their odd conversation.

Lottie shook her head. "When I was out for a ride, I saw him, standing in the water, staring out into the River Thames," her mother revealed. "He was wracked with grief at the loss of his wife, poor soul."

"Was this before you married Father?"

"Oh, no, it was after," her mother stated, matter-of-factly.

Surprised, Amelia lifted her brow.

Lottie sighed and continued, "I spent three unforgettable weeks with Lord Harrington, but it was many, many years ago."

Stopping at an open door, Aunt Nellie said, "We have arrived at your room, Lottie. Why don't you go lie down, and I will send up some refreshment?"

Her mother nodded before disappearing into her room. After a moment, Amelia ventured, "I am sorry about my mother. She doesn't appear very lucid right now."

"Don't be," Aunt Nellie assured her in a low voice. "Lottie and I are dear friends, but my heart is troubled by her aging body and mind." Her eyes trailed towards the open door. "I am just grateful that you called beforehand to explain her condition. She has aged considerably since her last visit to us two years ago."

Tightening her hold on the handles of the suitcases, Amelia replied, "Mum was adamant about attending your Full Moon Ball this summer."

"Do you know why?"

Amelia smiled and shrugged one shoulder. "Something about the 'magic of the full moon'."

"Ah," Aunt Nellie responded, returning her smile. "At least there was a reason."

"Thank you for playing along…" Her voice trailed off as the smile dropped from her face. "She is dying, you know, and there is nothing I can do to save her."

Aunt Nellie gazed at her with compassion. "It is not your job to save your mother, dear child."

Emotions welled inside of Amelia as she pressed her lips together. "After my father died, Mum started aging rapidly." Her words were filled with raw pain. "I believe she is dying from a broken heart."

"That would not surprise me," Aunt Nellie admitted. "No fairy tale could rival your mother and father's love. From the moment they met, they were inseparable."

Tears pricked Amelia's eyes as she whispered, "Why isn't she fighting it for my sake?"

"Who says she's not?" Aunt Nellie asked with an uplifted eyebrow as they stopped at the next door. "Trust your mother's intentions. We have been friends for a long time now. What I love most about your mother is her fierce loyalty to those whom she loves." Nellie wrapped her young friend in a motherly embrace, smelling of cinnamon and a light floral perfume.

"Thank you for that," Amelia murmured, appreciative of Aunt Nellie's insight.

"Why don't you have a quick lie-down, and I will send in your lady's maid, all right?"

"That does sound lovely," Amelia said, stifling a yawn as she turned to walk into her room. "It appears that I am more tired than I care to admit."

She pushed the suitcases up against the wall, tossed her shoes off and was asleep before her head hit the down-filled pillow.

Laura Beers

Chapter 2

Waking a couple of hours later to the smell of an applewood fire behind the polished brass, Amelia sat up in her large, ornately-carved, four-poster bed. Her yawn turned into a squeak when she saw a young, raven-haired woman with large, expressive eyes, dressed in a Regency-style maid's uniform, standing beside the bed.

"Good evening, Miss Wright," the maid said in a cheery voice. "My name is Marie. I'll be acting as your lady's maid during your stay at Twickenham Manor."

"Hello, Marie," she greeted back. "It's nice to meet you."

Marie tapped a finger over her lips, eyeing Amelia thoughtfully. "Time to prepare you for the ball, Miss. It takes a fair bit of time, it does."

Instead of being offended, Amelia decided to laugh it off. "Well, we'd best get started then."

After being poked, prodded, swathed, and coiffed for more than an hour, Amelia was at last dressed in a deep-green, empire-waisted gown with a rounded neckline and gold piping along the bottom. She had refused to wear the corset, insisting her own undergarments were sufficient, much to Marie's dismay.

Small flowers were scattered among the smooth, brown tresses that were now piled high on top of her head. Long curls framed her oval face, setting off her startling green eyes and accenting their amber flecks.

Glancing in the mirror, Amelia saw that her minimal makeup had been removed and replaced with a safflower-colored rouge on her lips and lightly-freckled cheeks. That was one added benefit to the Regency era, she thought. Natural beauty was encouraged. Between her medical duties, and caring for her ailing mother, she had little time to worry about her skin-care regimen.

There was a knock on the door. "Come in!" she shouted.

Marie gave her a stern look. "Ladies do not shout, Miss Wright," she chastised. "Nor do they encourage strangers to enter their rooms."

Stifling a smile, she replied, "My apologies."

Marie opened the door, and Lottie entered the room. She stopped when she spotted her daughter. "Oh, Amelia. You look beautiful!"

Turning in a circle, Amelia laughed as the gown billowed around her legs. "I do believe that the dresses become more elaborate each time we visit."

"I have your shoes, Miss," Marie said, holding out a pair of green slippers.

Putting her hand up in a gesture of refusal, Amelia replied, "I will not be wearing ballet flats all night to dance."

"Beggin' your pardon, but what will you wear?" Marie questioned, eyebrows raised.

Walking over to the door, Amelia picked up the strappy, tan wedges she had worn into Twickenham Manor. "No one will even see my shoes under this dress," she contended as she sat on the bed to fasten them on.

"Aunt Nellie will not be pleased," Marie mumbled under her breath.

Finding humor in Marie's criticism, Amelia did not think that Nellie would even mind. As much as she loved the Full Moon Ball, she did not enjoy dancing on a hardwood floor with thin slippers. It brought back memories of the many times she'd sat on a chair in the corner, massaging her feet while she hid from her dancing instructor.

"That will be all, Marie," her mother stated sweetly.

Marie curtsied and offered Lottie a kind smile. "Thank you, Mrs. Wright. It's a pleasure to see you again," she expressed before turning back and narrowing her eyes at Amelia.

Once Marie had closed the door behind her, Amelia commented, "I don't think Marie is too impressed with my Regency Immersion dedication."

"Never mind, dear. Marie will be quite all right."

Amelia rose from her seat on the eiderdown duvet. "I didn't realize you knew her."

"She has been my lady's maid many times before."

"Really? I don't remember her," Amelia admitted.

Her mother walked to the open window and looked out. "I love how the full moon sparkles over the Thames," she sighed. "It's ever so magical."

Reaching for her reticule, Amelia asked, "Are you ready to go to the ball, Mum?"

"Not quite yet. Before we go," Lottie said as she stepped across the antique silk rug, "I have a necklace that I would like you to wear tonight." She reached into her own reticule and pulled out a single-strand coral necklace, extending it towards her daughter.

Accepting the necklace, Amelia fingered the polished stones. "This is beautiful! Why haven't I seen it before?"

"Lord Harrington gave it to me as a token of his appreciation for our friendship." Her mother sighed again. "I couldn't very well wear a necklace that was given to me by another man, now could I?"

"I don't understand, Mum." Amelia shook her head, placing the necklace down on the bed. "When did you ever know a Lord Harrington?"

"Pay attention, Amelia," her mother ordered sharply, surprising her daughter with her intensity. "I promised Adam Baxter, the Earl of Harrington, that I would send someone back to help him, and you are just the person for the job." She reached up and placed a hand on Amelia's cheek affectionately. "It is time for your own adventure to begin."

Swallowing the lump in her throat, Amelia tried her best not to show how much her mother's delusional state saddened her. "Mum, did you forget to take your evening meds?"

"Never mind the pills. I am quite lucid," her mother declared in a steady voice. "You are about to embark on a grand adventure. I need you to understand that it may hurt, but the effects are only temporary."

"What will hurt?" Amelia asked, stepping over to her medical bag on the nightstand.

"Time travel."

Frowning, Amelia reached into her medical bag, removing her stethoscope and blood pressure cuff. This was a familiar delusion. She tried not to sound as frustrated with the topic as she felt. "Why would time travel hurt?"

Lottie placed a hand to her forehead. "When I time traveled, I would get the most intense headaches. I hope your body will sustain it better."

"Time travel isn't real," Amelia reminded her mother for the hundredth time.

"It is!" her mother insisted. "Every time we came to Twickenham Manor, I would travel to another time. It was incredible!"

Amelia tried to listen to her mother's heart, but Lottie swatted away the stethoscope.

"Mum, we used to take those trips as families, and you never left our side," Amelia informed her patiently, hoping to bring her mother back into the present.

"That's right," Lottie said. "Because Nellie always brought me back to the precise moment that I left," she paused, smiling, "give or take an hour or so."

Opening the blood pressure cuff, Amelia attempted to place it on her mother's upper arm, but Lottie would not cooperate. "How exactly did you time travel?"

"Aunt Nellie painted a portrait of me with the magic dew. It's hanging up on the fourth floor. I time traveled through my mural."

Perhaps she fell and had a concussion, Amelia thought, as she tried to look at her mother's pupils. "You must be confused. The fourth floor is off-limits to guests because that is where they store the period costumes."

Her mother spun in a circle, appearing younger than her seventy-two years of age. "That is what Nellie wanted you all to think."

"Are you referring to Aunt Nellie, the proprietress of Twickenham Manor?"

"Yes," her mother answered, her brow lifted. "Only she is not just a proprietress, she is the Matron of the Manor. She oversees all the magic."

"I see," Amelia said, deciding to play along. "Aunt Nellie is a fairy godmother."

Her mother smiled victoriously. "Exactly."

Sighing, Amelia placed everything back into her medical bag. "And you can only time travel at Twickenham Manor?"

"Yes, but only on a full moon," her mother corrected.

Reaching for the coral necklace, Amelia placed it over her head. "Did you meet Lord Harrington while time traveling?"

Her mother put her hand to her mouth. "Yes, but when I went back to visit him again, it had been almost six years later." She smiled. "As Aunt Nellie would say, time is a fuzzball."

Amelia embraced her mother warmly, sadly acknowledging to herself that she'd become delusional. "I love you, Mum."

"I love you, too," her mother replied, her expression growing serious. "This is important, Amelia." Her right hand cupped her daughter's cheek. "Two years ago, after your father died, I traveled back to see my dear friend, Lord Harrington, but I knew he wouldn't recognize me. I had grown too old, you see." The sadness in her eyes was palpable. "I promised Adam that I would help him, but he must feel that I've abandoned him by now. I need you to go and see to it that he is happy. Promise me that you will seek him out and help him," she pled.

Tears of frustration pricked at the back of Amelia's eyes. "You aren't making any sense."

Patting her cheek affectionately, her mother said, "It will all make sense soon. Come along, dear. It's time you saw your portrait on the fourth floor."

Amelia's jaw dropped. "There is a portrait of me here? In the manor?"

Her mother nodded with excitement. "Yes. Before I returned home, I commissioned Aunt Nellie to paint it. It is right next to mine."

Knowing she could not deny her mother's wish, Amelia sighed, "All right, Mum. We'll go look at the portraits, but then we'll go to the ball. Okay?"

Walking up the two flights of marble stairs was arduous for Lottie, and the two women had to stop multiple times so she could catch her breath. Once they reached the landing, she began leaning into her daughter for support.

"Are you all right?" Amelia asked with concern, sliding her own satin-gloved arm through her mother's.

"Don't fuss over me, Amelia," came her mother's usual reply.

Lottie stopped at an open door, slipped her arm out of Amelia's, and took small steps into the thickly-carpeted room. The lights were on, and Amelia followed closely behind. Standing towards the middle of the room, her mother indicated the portraits on the wall. Following her mother's gaze, Amelia saw a large painting that looked just like her mother as a younger woman. But then, beside it, hung Amelia's own uncanny likeness!

"Go on, my dear," her mother encouraged her. "Touch your portrait."

"This is remarkable," Amelia murmured, taking a few steps closer, admiring the beautiful brushstrokes. In the portrait, she was dressed in a white, empire-waist gown with her hair parted down the middle and wispy bangs curled around her face, but it was the smile that held Amelia transfixed. It lit up her face and gave the illusion that she was truly happy.

"I see you've found your portrait, Amelia," Aunt Nellie observed, coming up behind them, seemingly out of nowhere.

"Have fun," her mother said, the sound of her voice echoing as if from down a long tunnel.

A bright light erupted from behind Amelia, but before she could turn around, she felt as though her body was being used as a battering ram.

Chapter 3

May 1813

Amelia found herself thrown onto a carpet, tumbling to the floor. Her ears rang something fierce, and she felt a bit nauseous. What had just happened? Was that an explosion?

Moving slowly to a sitting position, her eyes roamed the wide room. A door and a large window faced each other on opposite walls, and the space in between them was covered with portraits. She stood up shakily and adjusted her skirt.

Turning around, she saw her mother's portrait as well as her own. Moving till she stood in front of her portrait, she reached to touch it, but a voice behind her stopped her. "I wouldn't touch that just yet, my dear. You might not return from whence you came."

Whirling around, Amelia saw Aunt Nellie scurrying towards her.

"Amelia, at last you have arrived!" the woman said, relief evident in her voice. "We have been waiting for you for two years."

"I don't understand," Amelia admitted in confusion. "My mother and I have been here all afternoon. You greeted us yourself, don't you remember? Mum and I came up to look at her portrait and..." she turned back to look at the portrait of herself, "then I stood next to this."

The woman gave her a kind smile and held out a hand, beckoning Amelia to come closer. "Amelia, my dear, it's true that I am Aunt Nellie, and you are at Twickenham Manor. But you are no longer *when* you think you are. When you touched your portrait, you traveled backward in time."

"What? That's impossible!" Amelia proclaimed. "This isn't making any sense. People do not just time travel through a portrait."

"Ah, but they can, as long as I have painted it. When I create a portrait, you see, it becomes a portal that allows the subject to travel to other eras. You have time traveled," Nellie declared simply. "You have arrived in the year 1813."

Amelia's mouth opened in disbelief. "Is this some type of a joke?" She looked around the room. "Am I on some type of reality show?"

"No, my dear, you are just overwhelmed." Aunt Nellie started leading her towards the door. "Let's get you some tea, and this will all begin to make sense."

"Do you have any soda?" she asked. "I am not a huge fan of English tea."

Nellie led her down a large hallway where more portraits lined the walls. "I am afraid that soda, as you know it, has yet to be invented."

Descending the marble staircase to the second floor, Amelia trailed behind the woman who called herself Aunt Nellie. The papered walls held bright, bold colors and gold, ornate ceilings ran down the lengths of the main halls. As always, the walls were dominated by large, beautiful portraits, and the hand-carved tables were decorated with expensive Chinese vases and porcelain knick-knacks. This was definitely

Twickenham Manor, but everything seemed different. How was that possible?

Entering the drawing room, Amelia lowered herself onto the settee. She looked out the window and saw green trees and fields surrounding the manor. But gone were all the familiar landmarks of the twenty-first century. This didn't make any sense.

"Tea, miss?" asked a maid's voice in front of Amelia, breaking her out of her musings.

"No, thank you," she declined, placing a hand to the stomach of her green dress. "My stomach is feeling out of sorts."

Nellie sat down next to her. "Amelia, dear, I'm afraid I must insist that you drink the tea."

"Why?" she asked warily.

Taking a cup herself, Nellie explained, "It is my own special recipe. I have developed it in order to combat the effects of time travel. It will settle your stomach and soothe your headache in no time."

She reached out and accepted the tea. "Thank you," she said, sniffing the tea cautiously.

Nellie went on, "It is a concoction of herbs with a pinch of something extraordinary."

Hesitantly, Amelia raised the cup to her lips. As the warm liquid went down her throat, she found herself beginning to relax. "Mmm. This is delicious!"

Once she was finished, Nellie reached for her cup and saucer and placed it on the table. "Now you'll find it easier to understand everything, my dear. Twickenham Manor is an ancient home constructed by fairie folk, or fae, to cover the fissure in the earth that had allowed their magic to seep into the human world," Nellie explained. "The magic leaks up out of the ground a little bit and settles as dew on the lawn and plants around the manor."

Amelia's eyes grew wide. "Aunt Nellie, I-I'm a doctor! I believe in science, not magic. And here you are, telling me that there is *magic* in the *ground?*"

Nellie laughed softly and adjusted the folds of her long, mauve skirt. "You seem to have focused on the magic portion of the story, but there is so much more. The fae and I gather the dew, and I use it to paint the portraits that are needed for time travel."

"And I suppose people time travel all the time through these portraits?"

"No. Visitors can only time travel on full moons," Nellie shared, "but it is not an exact science. Sometimes the magic burps and seems to have a mind of its own."

Amelia frowned. "What does that mean?"

"Well, for example, you were expected here two years ago." Nellie shrugged. "But time is a fuzzball, and we really can't pinpoint exact arrivals for everyone. One thing is clear, however; the magic placed you here, at this time, for a specific purpose."

"Which is?"

Nellie smiled. "I suppose we will find out together."

Amelia felt her head spin with all these far-fetched explanations. Rubbing her temples, she replied, "But two years ago, I had just started residency. Father had..." She swallowed a painful lump of memory, "had just died. And Mum suddenly made an unexpected pilgrimage here, to Twickenham Manor, alone. I thought it was her way of dealing with her grief." Amelia turned her head sharply to face the sympathetic woman who seemed at once so familiar and so strange. "Are you truly the same Aunt Nellie, or are you a distant relative of hers?"

"I am the very same," Nellie paused with a sweeping, inclusive wave of her hand, "but the future holds an older version of me."

"You look exactly the same."

Nellie beamed. "Excellent. That bodes well for me."

"How is this all possible?"

Reaching for Amelia's hand, Nellie's compassionate eyes rested upon her. "Eight years ago, your mother, Charlotte Wright, stepped through her portrait for the first time and came to visit us. While she was here, she avoided the balls and social gatherings, and instead, opted to ride around our lands and meet with other bluestockings, including Jane Austen. On one of her rides, she met our dear neighbor, Lord Harrington, who had just lost his wife, leaving behind a precious newborn baby girl."

"My mother mentioned a Lord Harrington, and she said she made him a promise."

"She did," Nellie confirmed. "Their friendship was not romantic in nature, because Lord Harrington was grieving the loss of his wife, and your mother was married. But they shared a special connection nonetheless."

Touching the coral necklace at her throat, Amelia asked, "Did he give her this necklace?"

"He did," Nellie acknowledged, holding out her hand. "May I?" As she fingered the coral, she continued her story. "When they met on the final day of her last visit, your mother told Lord Harrington that she had to leave, but she promised she would send him someone to help him with his grief."

"But it has been eight years," Amelia protested. "Surely, Lord Harrington has moved past it by now."

Releasing the necklace, Nellie shook her head. "Sadly, my dear neighbor has fallen further into despair, and his poor child has been raised in a home filled with sadness."

"I don't mean to be insensitive, but what does this have to do with me?"

"After your mother returned back to your time, she continued to visit us many times through the years. Each time, Charlotte aged with grace and dignity, but after the last visit, she knew that her advancing age would cause him too much shock. She shared with me her lifelong joy of being a wife and a mother, but her smile faded when I spoke of her friend, Adam, the Earl of Harrington. It was then that she gave me a miniature image of you." Nellie put a finger beneath Amelia's chin and lifted it, meeting the younger woman's troubled gaze with a frank and earnest expression.

"So, you created a portrait of me based on a photograph?"

"I did, which is why you are here," Nellie paused, smiling, "albeit two years later than we expected."

"Again, why me?" Amelia implored. "Why did my mother want to send me?"

"You were born to travel through time, my dear." At Amelia's baffled expression, Nellie continued to explain. "Your mother traveled here when she was expecting you, and the magic passed to you in the womb. That is how you came to be here. The future me assisted you along your journey."

Amelia remained silent, not knowing what to say, and Aunt Nellie gave her a tender smile. "Furthermore, your mother was able to help Lord Harrington see past himself. She felt confident that you would be able to help in the same way."

"And if I can't?"

Rising, Nellie smoothed out her gown. "Then you can return home on the next full moon, and you won't have to give Lord Harrington another moment of your time."

Taking her cue, Amelia rose and asked, "Won't people recognize that I am not of this time period?"

"I assume that in the future, I have taught you the stringent ways of our culture and customs?"

She nodded, so Aunt Nellie said, "Excellent, then we will get you dressed, and you can attend your first ball."

"But I am already dressed for a ball," Amelia objected, smoothing her gown.

"Yes, but not as appropriately as you should be," Nellie pointed out, indicating Amelia's shoes. She exited the room, Amelia following in her wake. "Currently, all the other guests are at supper, so I must not dally any longer." Increasing her stride, she continued, "If anyone asks, we will inform them that you were raised in the American colonies but recently returned to London to visit relations. Sadly, your reception might be a little chilly because of the anti-American sentiment right now."

"Is that because England is at war with the Americans?" Amelia asked, moving at a brisk pace as she attempted to keep up with Nellie.

Looking impressed, Nellie nodded. "Precisely. But you will discover that we use the term 'skirmish' in England, not 'war'. The true war is being fought on the peninsula."

Amelia nodded. She was well-versed on the War of 1812. She recalled many reasons America declared war on England, the greatest being the Royal Navy's habit of impressing American merchant sailors into service for the Crown. A thought occurred to her. She had a unique opportunity here. She could speak to the patrons at the ball and learn firsthand their thoughts on the war. This is a once-in-a-lifetime experience, she thought.

As if reading her mind, Nellie interrupted her musings. "As a reminder, Amelia, ladies never discuss politics, war, or business."

She stared at Nellie in surprise. Could she read her thoughts?

When Nellie didn't answer her unspoken question, Amelia assured her, "I remember the training. Regency ladies are limited to the subjects of fashion, gossip, and highlighting their many accomplishments."

"Excellent. Your memory will save us some time." Nellie stopped in front of a closed door. "This is your room. I will send Marie to serve as your lady's maid."

"Wait!" Amelia exclaimed as Nellie turned to leave.

"Is there a problem?"

"Mum's health is ailing," Amelia pleaded. "What if she dies while I am here in the past?"

Giving her an understanding smile, Nellie explained, "On the next full moon, I will send you back only moments after you first left your mother."

"What if the magic burps again?" Amelia asked nervously. "Will I return two or three years in the future?"

"Try not to worry." Nellie smiled reassuringly. "Returning you to your time should not be a problem. I admit that your arrival two years late was *odd*, but that was an anomaly. People travel back and forth through the ley lines without difficulty all the time."

"What exactly are 'ley lines'?"

"Ley lines are the mystical passageways between the Fae world and the human world. In the Fae world, magic abounds, and time doesn't have the same rules as you know it."

"Thank you," she said, feeling somewhat relieved.

Nellie started to leave but turned back. "It is a pleasure to have you, Miss Wright. I think we are going to be fast friends."

"Thank you, Aunt Nellie." Remembering the etiquette training she was put through at Twickenham Manor, she dipped into a low curtsy. However, when Amelia rose, she stumbled back and put her hand up on the wall to steady herself.

Stifling a smile, Nellie gave her a polite nod. "Why don't you practice your curtsy before dinner?"

"Yes, Aunt Nellie."

As she stepped inside her room, Amelia tried to make sense of what she'd been told. Time travel? She couldn't quite wrap her head around it. It went against everything she knew to be true. How was this possible? There must be a logical explanation. Was she dreaming? Hallucinating? Had she hit her head and...

Perhaps she was overthinking it. Maybe this was just the adventure she needed.

Good heavens, what was in that tea that made her so accepting of all this? It was all so ludicrous. Wasn't it?

Now wearing more appropriate attire, Amelia was dressed in a chemise, tight-laced stays, a long, white petticoat, silk stockings, and a white, muslin gown with a square neckline.

Running her hand down her gown, she felt the pink, embroidered flowers running the length of the dress.

Her hair was pinned low to one side, and tendrils had been curled to frame her face. To add to the grandeur, Marie, her lady's maid, had woven small pink flowers through her hair.

Amelia had established that it was the same Marie that was acting as her lady's maid in the future, but she appeared more relaxed here. Marie's special talent was creating flattering hairstyles, and both women stood before the elaborate gold floor-length mirror, admiring the maid's handiwork.

Marie broke through her reverie. "Miss Wright."

Turning her head, she saw Marie holding up white slippers. "Surely, you do not expect me to wear slippers all night to dance," she declared. Again?

"Slippers are worn to balls, Miss," Marie replied, shrugging.

Amelia accepted the silk shoes and balanced herself on one foot as she put them on. "Has the ballroom always been in the same location?" she asked.

"I should hope so, Miss! The ballroom has the most beautiful view of the River Thames."

As she approached the door, Amelia stopped and asked, "Can you throw some magic dew on me to make me a good dancer?"

Marie laughed. "The magic does not work that way. Only Aunt Nellie has control over the magic."

"It appears that I am left to my own devices then."

"Good luck, Miss Wright."

Smiling, she said, "Thank you. I am going to need all the luck I can get."

As she descended the stairs, voices drifted up to meet her accompanied by the musical cacophony of an orchestra warming up. She stepped into the ballroom and saw elegantly dressed men and women chatting merrily to each other.

Respectful of the Regency customs, Amelia stayed near the back of the room, hoping Aunt Nellie would eventually take heed of her and introduce her to a few of the patrons. Until then, she would enjoy observing her first *real* Regency ball.

As her eyes drifted over the crowd, a few heads turned her way, but no one gave her much notice. She caught a few gentlemen staring at her, but they quickly turned away when she met their gaze. Furthermore, she almost giggled when she saw a few ladies stick their noses up at her.

A few moments later, Aunt Nellie approached her, wearing a stunning gold gown, and matching flowered headpiece.

"Are you enjoying yourself?" Nellie asked.

Amelia leaned closer to her so her words couldn't be overheard. "I am not used to being ostracized."

"Well, you are an American on English soil, and we are technically at war," Nellie reminded her.

"How would anyone know that?" Amelia questioned. "No one has approached me."

Nellie grinned. "At dinner, I announced that I had an American guest, and I heard a few people murmuring their disapproval."

"I guess I won't be dancing with the Prince of Wales tonight," Amelia joked, trying to cover her nervousness.

Aunt Nellie laughed softly. "Prinny is not attending our ball tonight."

Amelia stood on her tiptoes to look over the heads of all the patrons in the crush. "Is Lord Harrington in attendance?"

"No, he hasn't attended one of my social gatherings since his wife died."

"Perhaps I should just go back upstairs," she said. "I wouldn't want any of your guests to feel uncomfortable around me, since I am an American."

"Nonsense," Aunt Nellie declared. "Give me one moment." Her eyes scanned the room, widening with anticipation. "If you will excuse me." With those words, her only friend disappeared into the crowded ballroom.

Without warning, the voices quieted. Everyone seemed to stop talking at once, and all their eyes shifted towards her. Women put their fans up and whispered back and forth to each other. Just moments before, she'd had no one's attention, and now she commanded the room. What just happened?

Aunt Nellie appeared beside her, practically beaming. "Smile," she encouraged under her breath. "I just told a few busybodies that you are an heiress from America and that your wealth rivals the Duke of Albany's."

"I highly doubt that," Amelia demurred, knowing that she would be entitled to a small fortune once her mother passed away. It was a fortune she would freely give up if it meant they could have more time together.

"Come now," Aunt Nellie said, looping her arms through Amelia's. "Let me introduce you to a few gentlemen."

Chapter 4

Entering the dining room where a breakfast buffet was being served, Amelia was surprised to see a young lady already eating at the long table.

"Good morning," she greeted cheerfully.

The beautiful brown-haired woman with olive skin swiveled in her chair. "Are you a time traveler as well, or a fae?"

"I am a time traveler."

"Good," she said, exhaling loudly. "Last night, I was here for a ball, only in the year 2018, and then I decided to go exploring."

Reaching for a plate, Amelia helped herself to some food before she joined the girl. "Let me guess," she paused, dramatically, "you went up to the fourth floor and saw your portrait."

"Yes," the excitable woman exclaimed. "Then poof!"

"I do apologize for that, but the magic burped and pulled you in," Aunt Nellie explained as she entered the room. "We were not expecting you, but we are pleased that you came to visit us." She took a seat at the table. "The portrait you saw in your time has not yet been created. I will paint it before the next full moon."

"I did not catch your name," Amelia said, placing her napkin on her lap.

"My name is Peyton," the woman answered, "but I don't think that is a normal Regency-era name."

"It's not," Aunt Nellie confirmed, "but you will only be here till the next full moon."

"My name is Amelia," she offered.

Peyton used her fork to move her food around. "What do you have planned today?" she asked Amelia.

Wiping her mouth with her napkin, she replied, "I plan to call on Lord Harrington."

Aunt Nellie took a deep breath, placed her teacup down and looked at Amelia sternly. "You can't just call on a gentleman, dear. It's not proper."

"I don't even have a full month till the next full moon. During that time, I have to establish a friendship with Lord Harrington and help him find a way to overcome his grief. Then I can go back home and help ease my mother's conscience," Amelia explained. "Naturally, the best course of action is to march up to his estate and request an audience with him."

"I see," Aunt Nellie murmured, amusement clearly on her features. "And if he refuses to see you? You would be an unaccompanied lady, after all."

Amelia shrugged. "Then I will show him the coral necklace, and he will agree to see me."

"What do you intend to say?" Aunt Nellie asked, reaching for a bowl of jam.

Amelia drummed her fingers on the table before saying, "I believe it will come to me when I meet him."

"I would be happy to go along with you and provide an introduction," Aunt Nellie offered. "I have known Lord Harrington for many years."

Amelia shook her head. "I can handle the introduction. It will be best to get this awkward conversation over with."

"Your plan is far from flawless, and I can't even count how many ways it could go terribly wrong," Aunt Nellie teased. "However, I trust that you will find a way to get through to Lord Harrington." A smile came to her lips. "I will order the carriage for you."

"That's not necessary, Aunt Nellie. My lady's maid informed me that Lord Harrington's land borders your estate on the east. May I just borrow a horse?"

"You may. Do you know how to ride sidesaddle?" Aunt Nellie asked with an uplifted brow.

"I am a competent rider, but I have never used a sidesaddle before. It couldn't possibly be that difficult to figure out," she said, feeling fairly confident. Her mother had insisted that she take riding lessons from a young age.

Aunt Nellie smirked. "Have you ever ridden a horse in a dress?"

"No, I haven't," she admitted.

"Well, you are in for a treat, my dear," Aunt Nellie joked. "Fortunately, Lord Harrington's estate is easy to find. Belmont Manor is visible once you ride over the hill to the east."

Amelia smiled confidently. "I have a great sense of direction. I have no doubt that I will find my way easily."

Instead of responding, Aunt Nellie chuckled before she turned towards Peyton. "This will allow me to give you a tour of our lands."

A short time later, Amelia trotted her horse across the east field towards Belmont Manor, feeling elated that she'd picked up the knack for riding sidesaddle so easily. As she neared the main house, she admired the imposing, three-level manor.

Reining in her horse before she reached the cobblestone drive, she unhooked her right leg, removed her left foot out of the stirrup and slipped off. She hadn't practiced dismounting, though, and she fell to the ground, collapsing in a heap.

"That was graceful," she mumbled as she dusted herself off.

A small giggle came from behind a tree. Turning her head towards the noise, Amelia saw a young girl with brown hair arranged in a loose chignon watching her curiously.

Amelia smiled. "I was hoping no one would witness my first attempt at riding sidesaddle."

"Have you never ridden a horse before?" the girl asked as she placed her hand on the tree.

Leading her horse closer to the girl, she replied, "To be honest, I usually ride astride."

The girl's eyes grew wide with disbelief. "Like how the men ride?"

She nodded, adjusting her riding gloves. "It's much easier."

The girl inched closer to her, revealing a sprinkling of freckles on her nose and cheeks. "Are you here to apply for the governess position?"

Amelia shook her head. "No, I am here to speak to Lord Harrington."

"He's my father."

Rubbing her horse's neck, Amelia asked, "What's your father like?"

"He doesn't like me very much." The girl lowered her gaze.

Amelia's hand stilled, and she crouched next to the girl. "Why do you say that?"

The girl's sad eyes came up. "I look like my mother, and he loved her very much. But she is dead now."

"I am sorry for your loss," she murmured. "What's your name?"

"Marian."

"Well, Marian. My name is Amelia," she said, rising.

"Amelia?" she repeated in an excited tone. "Are you here to be my friend?"

"I would very much like to be your friend, Marian."

Marian waved her closer. "Please don't tell my father that I am outside unescorted. He gets mad when I sneak out of the estate."

"Won't your father notice you are gone?"

She shook her head. "No, he's very busy. At least, that's what he says. I think he's just very sad."

"So, who watches over you?"

"Mrs. Troxler watches me, but she fell asleep next to my bed. I am supposed to be resting." Marian put a hand next to her mouth and whispered, "You can't say anything, though. My father just fired my last governess because he found her lacking, and I don't want Mrs. Troxler to get fired. I like her. She is a nice maid and offered to care for me until a new governess could be employed."

Amelia pursed her lips, finding herself growing more irritated by this Lord Harrington. Bringing her gaze up towards the country home, she extended her hand. "How about I walk you inside?"

Marian smiled and placed her small hand into Amelia's own. "You possess an unusual manner of speaking, Miss Amelia."

Amelia grinned. "I suppose it is because I am from America."

"You came all the way from America?" Marian asked with wide eyes.

A groomsman approached them as they neared the main door, and Amelia handed off her horse. Smiling down at Marian, she replied, "I did."

Walking up to the main door, Amelia knocked loudly as Marian hid behind her skirt. The door opened, and a tall, heavy-set servant answered the door.

"May I help you?" he asked in an irritated huff.

"I am here to see Lord Harrington," she announced.

The man lifted his brow. "Is this regarding the position of the governess?"

"No, it is not." Amelia kept her back rigid and strengthened her resolve under the butler's scrutiny. "I have an urgent matter to discuss with him."

The butler's frown deepened, and it appeared he wanted to say more but opted to open the door, allowing her entry into the hall. "Do you have a calling card, Miss…" He let his words trail off.

"No, but you can tell him that my name is Miss Amelia Wright," she said as she removed her bonnet.

The butler strode away, and Marian came from behind her. "You made Mr. Blake angry."

"Why do you say that?" Amelia asked while looking around the spacious two-level entry hall.

The ceiling caught her eye first. It was painted with intricate designs which led her eye to the large, arched marbled columns separating several seating spaces. It was elegant and sophisticated, but the mood of the home seemed sad, depressing even.

The girl tugged at her braid. "It's all right. I make him angry all the time."

Mr. Blake's voice broke up their conversation. "Lord Harrington will see you now, Miss Wright. Follow me." His gaze turned towards Marian and softened. "Lady Marian, you are supposed to be resting in the nursery."

"Yes, Mr. Blake," Marian said, turning to give her a secretive smile. She turned to walk up the stairs, but Amelia had no doubt that she wouldn't go far.

Following Mr. Blake down an expansive hall, Amelia noticed the portraits grew larger and more ostentatious as they went. At the end of the hall, there was an open door, and the butler stopped and stepped aside, allowing her to enter.

As soon as she stepped into the room, Amelia saw a man not much older than she, standing behind a large, mahogany desk. Lord Harrington had dark brown hair, long sideburns, and a strong, square jaw. Besides being tall, he had broad shoulders, blue eyes, and was by far the most attractive man she had ever met. For a moment, she forgot about her purpose for being there.

"Miss Amelia Wright, I presume," the deep, baritone voice said, drawing her back into the present.

"You would be correct," she answered, then, remembering Regency etiquette, she offered Lord Harrington a curtsy and murmured, "my lord."

Before she even brought her head back up, he snapped his fingers. "Bring me your references."

She gave him a blank look. "References?"

"Past employers, relatives, things of that nature," Lord Harrington listed, not bothering to hide his annoyance. "Do you not have any?"

"I do not," she replied, "but that is not…"

He cut her off. "Have you had any schooling?"

"Yes, I am quite educated." Amelia noticed the shelves on the opposite side of the room. They were stacked with books, and she desperately wanted to see what was in his collection.

"Are you from the American colonies?" he asked, his tone critical.

Reluctantly, she turned her gaze back to him. "I am from Boston."

Lord Harrington's eyes seemed to assess her, scowling. "Are you at least fluent in French or Latin?"

"I am not, but that has nothing…"

Lord Harrington sighed in exasperation as he sat down in his chair. "How many instruments can you play?"

Taking a step closer to the desk, Amelia offered him a polite smile. "As I have attempted to explain, I am not here…"

"How old are you?" he asked, speaking over her.

She lifted her chin in the air. "I am twenty-seven."

"No marriage prospects, then?" he asked gruffly. "Or has your family come on hard times?"

Amelia's eyes widened at his blatant rudeness. "That is none of your concern."

Leaning back in his seat, Lord Harrington sighed. "Why are you wasting my time, Miss Smythe?"

Did he just forget her name? "It is Miss Wright," she corrected.

He waved his hand dismissively. "My apologies, Miss." He lifted his brow. "I am a busy man, and I don't have time for cheeky American spinsters that have no qualifications to be a governess."

Amelia met his gaze, refusing to cower or step back from this bold, irritating man. Not only had she worked hard to be accepted into Harvard Medical school, but she had spent countless hours becoming the top resident in obstetrics. She would not be bullied by this pretentious British lord.

Squaring her shoulders, she prepared to do battle with this half-wit. "First of all, how dare you talk to me in such a degrading fashion. I came a long way to speak to you, and this is how you thank me?"

Lord Harrington rose from his chair, his eyes not wavering from her face. "You are in *my* home, and I will address you in any manner that I see fit."

"Now you are just being a ninnyhammer," she declared, immensely pleased that she remembered that British term correctly.

He reached down and shifted a few papers around on his desk. "Do you have any sort of decorum, Miss Armstrong?"

"Good heavens, you infuriating man!" she exclaimed. "My name is Amelia Wright. Not Miss Smythe. Not Miss Armstrong. *Amelia Wright.*"

"Thank you, Miss *Wright*," he emphasized. "That is all. You are dismissed."

Striding closer to the desk, she put her palms down and leaned closer to him. "You are nothing like what I imagined."

"And what exactly did you imagine me to be like?" he asked, giving her an annoyed look.

"A gentleman." Amelia removed her hands from the desk and straightened up. His eyes widened, but he did not respond, choosing to stare at her instead. "Good day, *my lord*," she drawled, her words dripping with contempt.

As she exited Lord Harrington's study, Amelia saw Marian sitting on the ground, her back up against the wall. Her sad, hazel eyes looked up at her. "You aren't going to be my governess, are you?"

She crouched down low to be closer to Marian. "I am sorry, sweetie. I truly hope your father finds you a nice governess."

"But I wanted *you* to be my governess." Marian's eyes filled with tears. "We were supposed to be friends, and you were going to help my father be happy."

For some reason, her heart lurched for this little girl. She had lost her mother, her father was an idiot, and her eyes testified of her loneliness.

Amelia placed her hand on Marian's shoulder. "I am staying not far from here at Twickenham Manor. Perhaps in a few days, I can ask your father to let us go on a ride together. Would you like that?" Marian nodded through her teary eyes. "Good." She rose. "Now, would you please escort me out to the stables? I have no idea where that groomsman put my horse."

"The stable is around back." Marian giggled, as Amelia hoped she would. The delightful sound made her heart rejoice.

She extended her hand and was pleased when Marian accepted it. Without so much as a glance backwards, the two walked down the hall towards the main door. They didn't see Lord Harrington watching them go, a bewildered expression on his face.

Adam, the Earl of Harrington, stood on the other side of the wall as he heard his daughter's tearful plea to Miss Wright. How was she able to speak to Marian with such ease and with such a teasing lilt in her voice? His daughter barely uttered a word around him. His staff attempted to appease his worry by telling him that she was just a quiet child. But now, she was chatting and giggling with Miss Wright. How was that possible?

Stepping outside of his study, he saw Miss Wright walking hand in hand with Marian, and they were still chatting merrily. His daughter may have wanted Miss Wright as her governess, but she was wholly unprepared for the job. Besides being an American, she did not speak French, nor did she have a civil tongue. No, his daughter would most definitely be better off without this cheeky American spinster.

If he was honest with himself, he was surprised that Miss Wright was even in his study. She was an exquisite woman with high cheekbones, dimpled cheeks, and full lips. Although her external loveliness was evident, her true attractiveness was in her eyes. They spoke of wit and intellect, causing him to forget himself and accidentally calling her by the wrong name... twice. How was a woman of such beauty not married?

Ignoring his reservations, he opened his mouth to call her back. Perhaps he was wrong to dismiss her so quickly.

"Miss Wright, a word, please," he called down the hall.

"No, thank you," she replied over her shoulder. "I don't wish to be insulted again."

Wait… did she just dismiss him? He was an earl, and she was… an American. He moved down the hall towards her. "I wish to discuss the governess position with you." There, that should make her happy.

"Even if I were destitute, living on the side of the road, I still would not work for you, Lord Harrington," she declared haughtily as Mr. Blake held open the door for them. Even more infuriating was that despite her sharp tone with him, she graciously tipped her head at his butler. "Thank you, Mr. Blake."

The butler smiled down at her. "You are welcome, Miss Wright."

"Wait!" Lord Harrington exclaimed, following her out the door. "Please, *stop*." That was the correct thing to say because Miss Wright stopped, but her back remained rigid, and her head was still held high.

She slowly turned around, and Marian went with her. "You wish to see me, *my lord*?" Her sharp words ground in his ears.

He pressed his lips tightly together. Did this woman possess any decorum? He turned his gaze towards his daughter. "Go inside, Marian. I need to speak to Miss Wright, alone."

Marian's wide, pleading eyes looked up at him. "Please, Father, may Miss Wright be my governess?"

"Go inside, Marian," he ordered, his voice rising. "This is none of your concern."

Miss Wright's eyes narrowed at his words, and her lips lowered in disapproval. Crouching down to eye-level with Marian, she continued to hold her hand. "What your father is attempting to say, though he's failing miserably," she paused, turning her heated gaze up at him, "is that he needs a moment to apologize to me for his horrifically rude behavior."

Marian's eyes shifted towards him. She brought a hand up alongside her mouth and whispered, "My father doesn't apologize. He says it is a sign of weakness."

Lord Harrington could see Miss Wright tense, and her lips were pressed so tightly together that they turned white. "Is that so?" She brought her hand up and placed it on Marian's shoulder. "Why don't you go inside and ask for a biscuit?"

Marian nodded sadly, and it tore at her father's heartstrings. Without sparing him a glance, his daughter walked back towards the main door.

Miss Wright rose and dusted off her skirt as they watched Marian enter the manor. Being conscious that there were prying eyes on them, Lord Harrington gestured away from the house, indicating that they should take a walk.

He clasped his hands behind his back. "Marian doesn't normally speak to others."

Fingering the strings of the bonnet in her hand, Amelia replied, "She is a beautiful little girl. How old is she?"

"She just turned eight." Lord Harrington kept his eyes straight ahead. "My wife passed away after giving birth to Marian, and I found myself wallowing in grief. Whenever I look at Marian, I see my Agnes. They have the same face, the same eyes…" His voice trailed off as he stopped. "I am embarrassed to admit it, but Marian has been barely an afterthought, even after all these years."

Miss Wright's face had softened as he shared his story. "I understand the complexities of grief, Lord Harrington, but I think you are a fool to have wasted these past eight years with your daughter. Time is fleeting, and you never know when a loved one will be taken from you."

"You seem to speak from experience," he observed. "Have you lost someone close to you?"

She nodded. "My father. He was taken from me in a horrible accident."

"A carriage accident?"

"No, but something similar."

He resumed walking. "My condolences for your loss."

Giving him a sad smile, she replied, "And I am sorry for your loss as well."

"I don't know why I am telling you all of this."

Miss Wright placed her bonnet back on her head and tied the strings loosely around her neck. "I have learned that the more you share a traumatic experience, the less hold it has on your physical and emotional reactions."

He cast her a puzzled expression. "Do all Americans speak as freely and as boldly as you?"

"I suppose so." Miss Wright smiled at him, revealing a set of perfectly white, straight teeth.

As they neared the stable, he said, "I overheard you tell Marian that you are staying at Twickenham Manor."

"It's true," she confirmed but was not forthcoming with any additional information.

"Are you related to Aunt Nellie?" he prodded.

"No, I am just visiting her."

"For how long?"

A groom walked Amelia's chestnut gelding out of the stable and approached them. Harrington stepped out and accepted the reins, dismissing the groomsman. He wanted to finish his conversation with Miss Wright in private.

She walked up to the horse and started petting its neck. "I intend to only stay for a month."

"What if I offered you the position of governess?"

Amelia shook her head, a wistful expression coming over her. "It would not change. I am needed at home."

Lord Harrington cast his eyes towards his estate and said, "I find that I am in the unique position of begging you to stay."

She dropped her hand from the horse and faced him. "I did not come here to apply for the governess position."

"Then why did you come?" he asked, taking a step closer to her. Why was he so drawn to this woman, this stranger?

"I was sent by someone who cared about you very much."

The sadness in her tone made him think there was more to the story. "Have we met before?"

She shook her head. "No, this is my first time to your estate."

When his eyes met hers, he said, "I will pay you £50 a year to stay on as Marian's governess." That should do it, he thought. It was a generous wage, and he had learned that money solved any problem.

Evidently, that was the wrong thing to say, because Amelia's eyes turned fiery. "I do not want, nor need, your money, Lord Harrington," she said dryly as her left hand reached for the reins. "I wish you luck finding a governess, but it won't be me."

Reaching out, he placed his hand on her sleeve. "Wait, don't go, please." Immediately, recognizing the impropriety of the situation, he dropped his hand and stepped back. "Perhaps you could spend some time with Marian tomorrow and help me select a suitable governess for her?" He attempted to keep the plea out of his voice, but he found he didn't want this Miss Wright to simply ride off without a commitment.

Several emotions played across Amelia's face. It seemed clear that her resolve was weakening, so he added, "Please teach me how to converse with my daughter as freely as you do."

After a long moment, Amelia's mouth started curling upward, causing him to focus on her lips. "I propose an arrangement of sorts," she said, her eyes growing mischievous. "I will do as you ask, provided you are willing to have some fun."

"I beg your pardon?" He grinned. "Will you please refrain from using your American idioms when you speak to Marian? After all, she is a lady."

Amelia's smile grew wide, causing his chest to swell with an unfamiliar emotion. "I will see you tomorrow, then." She put her left foot into the stirrup, and her right hand reached up to hold the saddle. As she hopped up, she missed the saddle and slid back down.

"May I assist you?" he offered, attempting to hold back his laughter.

She turned to face him with a blush on her cheeks. "It was much easier when the groom assisted me this morning."

Lord Harrington put his hands down low, so she could step into them with her left foot. He boosted her easily up into the saddle; then he politely averted his gaze while she adjusted her skirts. As she tightened her hold on the reins, he smiled up at her.

"I look forward to seeing you tomorrow."

"Good day, Lord Harrington," she said before she rode away.

Turning his head towards the stable, he saw his stable master watching him. He tipped his head towards the departing American lady, indicating that he wanted someone to trail behind to ensure her safety. The stable master nodded and disappeared inside to saddle another horse and do his master's bidding.

At the top of a small hill, Miss Wright turned back and waved. He raised his arm in response and smiled. The muscles around his lips felt strained, and he realized this was the first time he had truly smiled or laughed in eight years.

Laura Beers

Chapter 5

Entering Aunt Nellie's drawing room, Amelia was pleased to find Peyton sitting in a chaise lounge, next to the large bay window, reading a book. "Good morning," she greeted her, sitting down next to her. "Where did you go last night?"

Peyton placed the book down and turned to face her. "After touring the lands, Aunt Nellie secured invitations to a ball."

"Did you have fun?"

"It was magical." She smiled slyly. "I danced with handsome lords all night, and Lord Wessex even asked me to take a stroll around the gardens."

Feeling a need to tease her newfound friend, Amelia put her hand up to her head, feigning shock. "A stroll around the gardens. Good heavens, what's next? Your engagement?"

Peyton laughed. "Perhaps I should tell these stiff lords about my last date."

Amelia grinned. "Now you have piqued my interest, but you should be warned that it couldn't have been worse than mine. My date took me to Taco Bell."

"Taco Bell?" Peyton repeated, amusement in her eyes.

"It was classy," Amelia joked, laughing.

Holding up a finger, Peyton started, "Let's see, for starters, my date picked me up in an Uber car. He said he didn't want to lose his parking spot in front of his apartment complex."

She held up a second finger. "Second, my date took me to Chili's but went to the bathroom for almost twenty minutes when the check arrived."

"Did you end up paying?"

Peyton nodded. "I did, but he did pay for the McDonald's ice cream cones that we ate while walking around his neighborhood." She smirked. "In fact, he had the audacity to ask me if I preferred a regular cone or a kiddie cone, which was *free*."

"Oh, my," Amelia said, giggling. "That sounds romantic."

"It was," Peyton replied. "Which is why it is refreshing to be surrounded by true gentlemen." Picking up her book, she placed it on the table next to her. "Speaking of which, how did your meeting go with Lord Harrington?"

Amelia rolled her eyes. "He is the definition of a brooding lord," she huffed. "He is dashingly handsome, but he has the boorish personality of Mr. Darcy."

"What do you mean?"

"He is unfriendly, aloof, and extremely frustrating," Amelia listed. "He even called me the wrong name, not once, but twice."

"Really?" Peyton asked with an uplifted brow. "I take it that you won't be seeing him again."

A black carriage, with the top folded down, pulled up to Aunt Nellie's door. A uniformed driver sat in front with a whip in his hand, and another uniformed man sat next to him. Once the carriage rolled to a stop, the groomsman jumped down and walked towards the front door.

"What in the world?" Peyton asked. "Is this the Regency's version of an Uber ride?"

Amelia laughed at her friend. "I wonder who the carriage is for." Glancing back at the open door, she asked, "Do you suppose another time traveler made an appearance last night?"

"Actually, the barouche is here for you," Aunt Nellie declared as she entered the drawing room, her pink, muslin dress flowing behind her. "Lord Harrington even sent along a note."

Peyton eyed her with suspicion. "I thought you said Lord Harrington was boorish and rude."

"I did," she said, accepting the letter from Aunt Nellie. She unfolded the note and read:

> *Miss Wright,*
>
> *I know we did not specify a time for your arrival, but Marian has been asking for you since sunrise. When you are ready, please use my barouche to travel to the estate.*
>
> *With gratitude, your humble servant*
>
> *Adam Baxter, Earl of Harrington*

Taking the note, Amelia folded the paper and tucked it into her pocket. Aunt Nellie gave her an expectant look, so she spent the next few minutes sharing the details of her meeting with Lord Harrington.

She ended the story with, "I agreed to help him find a suitable governess for Marian."

Peyton jumped up from her seat in excitement. "What a fun adventure! Not only do you get to spend time with a handsome earl, but you are going to help him to become closer to his daughter."

Amelia rose and smoothed down her floral gown. She rather liked the puffy sleeves and green ribbon tied high on her waist. "That is precisely my plan."

Aunt Nellie chuckled. "And when exactly did you come up with that plan? Was this before or after he asked you to leave his estate?"

Laughing, she admitted, "It may have been as I was attempting to mount my horse. I was unable to get onto my side saddle without assistance." She shifted her gaze out the window, admiring the carriage, before turning back to Aunt Nellie. "Would it be permissible to drive to Lord Harrington's estate now?"

"Of course," Aunt Nellie replied, inclining her head. "Don't forget, tomorrow I am hosting a picnic on the lawn. It will be a grand affair. I had previously sent an invitation to Lord Harrington, but he has yet to respond. Would you mind personally inviting him?"

"Not at all," Amelia said as she exited the room. Not wasting any time, she went back to her room to retrieve a straw bonnet with green flowers.

Despite the rigid social customs, Amelia had to admit that she did enjoy the lovely gowns, hats, and accessories. They made her feel so... ladylike. Stopping at her dressing table mirror, she put the bonnet over her tight chignon, ensuring the curled tendrils of her hair were visible. When her lady's maid, Marie, had approached her with hot curling tongs, she had almost jumped out of her seat. However, Marie had curled her hair efficiently, without burning her neck.

As she came outside, the groomsman jumped off the barouche and opened the door to the carriage. "Miss Wright," he said, respectfully, as he proffered his hand to assist her inside.

Once seated comfortably, she clasped her hands together as the carriage jerked forward. A smile came to her lips. She could get used to this lifestyle.

The Earl of Harrington sat in his study and tapped the quill against the side of the ink pot, removing the excess ink. Bringing the quill back to the stack of papers in front of him, he began the process of signing his correspondence. This was the only life he had known, but it was not the life he had intended.

His father had passed away when Harrington was eight, and he'd inherited the earldom. His mother, along with the estate's bailiff, had worked tirelessly to keep the estate profitable while he was away at Oxford, but she had eventually succumbed to consumption. At the age of twenty, he'd found himself alone, despite being surrounded by servants and an entire village for which he was responsible.

Then, he had met Miss Agnes Hawkins at a country dance. She was a sweet girl that had stolen his heart from the moment she coyly agreed to accept his offer to dance. They had been blissfully happy for three glorious years, until it was time for Agnes to deliver Marian. The doctor was summoned after the midwife declared his wife's health was failing. Between them, they helped deliver Marian, but Agnes' lifeblood had drained away before his eyes.

Banishing his thoughts, Adam tossed the quill down on his desk and rubbed his eyes. Where had those memories come from? He had worked hard to suppress reminders of Agnes, so much that he had even distanced himself from his one living reminder, their only child. Yet, even now, the pain was still raw.

Reaching again for the quill, he heard laughter floating in from the open casement window. He glanced out the window and saw Miss Wright and Marian running towards a wooded section of his property. As they disappeared from his view, he made an impromptu decision to join them. He grabbed his coat from the back of his chair and started heading for the main door.

Mr. Blake met him at the door. "Miss Wright has arrived, my lord."

"Thank you, Blake," he replied, shrugging on his coat.

Opening the door, his butler asked, "Are you visiting the stables?"

He shook his head. "No, I intend to spend some time with my daughter."

"Very good, milord," Mr. Blake said, a minute smile on his lips.

Approaching the cluster of trees that he saw the girls disappear into, he heard laughter coming from within. "Five… four… three… two… one…," Miss Wright counted down. "I am coming to find you."

Holding up her dress so it wouldn't drag on the ground, Miss Wright began moving in a most unladylike pace around the trees. "Where are you, Lady Marian?"

Harrington heard giggling coming from above, and he turned his head up to see Marian hiding in the tree. She put her finger to her lips, then beckoned him to join her.

Why not? He hadn't climbed a tree in years! He reached up, grabbed the lowest branch and hoisted himself up. To his amazement, Marian snuggled up against him as they watched Miss Wright come closer.

"Lady Marian... where are you?" Miss Wright teased in a sing-song voice. Now, she was right below them.

Unable to contain her mirth, Marian giggled loudly but clapped her hand over her mouth to cover her laughter. Putting her finger to her lips, Amelia began tapping them as if deep in thought. "I wonder where Lady Marian is?" Tilting her head up, her smile grew wide as she found their hiding spot. "Well, look at that!" she exclaimed. "I found a lord and a lady sitting in a tree."

"It's your turn to hide, and I will seek," Marian declared as she scrambled down the tree. Turning towards the tree, she put her arms up and pressed her face into them. "Ten... nine..."

Miss Wright ran and ducked behind a massive oak tree. Jumping down, Adam attempted to tiptoe around his daughter, but dry leaves crunched under his boots.

"Five... four..." Marian continued.

Running stealthily towards Miss Wright's place of concealment, he joined the brash young American. "Go find your own tree," she whispered over her shoulder.

He grinned. "But I prefer this tree."

Placing her hand on the rough bark, she peeked out to look for Marian. "Where is she?"

"She's gone?"

Amelia looked back at him and whispered, "If you insist on hiding with me, Lord Harrington, then please, at least attempt to stand against the tree." She gave him a pointed look. "You are going to give away our position."

As bidden, he leaned closer to her against the gnarled trunk, enjoying the sweet scent of rosewater. "I didn't realize we were preparing for battle."

Her eyes twinkled with merriment. "One always prepares oneself for battle, my lord."

"Interesting," he said, rubbing his shaved chin.

"What's interesting?"

He dropped his hand. "I didn't think it was possible for you to address me without sounding condescending, Miss Wright."

Amelia shifted her position, so her back was against the tree. "It should not surprise you. I am actually quite a social person."

"Are you, now?" he asked, his eyes roaming her face.

"Found you!" Marian shouted suddenly, causing him to jump back in alarm.

Amelia watched him in amusement; then she turned towards Marian. "It appears that you scared your father witless."

Running a hand through his hair, Harrington felt a need to defend himself. "Not so! I knew she was there all along."

Rolling her eyes, Amelia just laughed. "All right, Lord Liar-Pants, it is your turn."

"What is a 'liar-pants'?" Marian asked.

Amelia put her hands on her knees and leaned closer to his daughter. "It is my new favorite nickname for your father," she replied with a teasing lilt.

Harrington sighed. "You are horrible at giving nicknames."

Straightening up, Amelia touched his sleeve. "Tag, you are it."

"What did you sa…" His words stilled when both Amelia and Marian ran in opposite directions, his daughter's laughter dancing in the wind.

For the next hour or so, they played this game of 'tag' in the woods but stopped when it became clear that his daughter was tiring.

Offering his arm to Miss Wright, he asked, "Would you like to join us for a midday meal?"

She accepted his arm with a dazzling smile. "I would be honored."

Ambling towards Belmont Manor with Miss Wright on his arm and his daughter running around them, he found his mood souring. What was he thinking, spending time with another woman? Did he dare disrespect his dear Agnes's memory?

Amelia stopped, withdrawing her arm from his. "What's wrong?"

"Nothing." His voice was sharper than he intended.

"You seem upset…"

"It's none of your concern, Miss Wright," he barked. "Pray, leave me in peace at once."

Shrinking away from him, the hurt was evident on her features.

Instead of the quick retort the earl anticipated, her face grew expressionless before she offered him a tentative smile. "I just remembered something," she said evenly. "Aunt Nellie asked me to come home for the midday meal."

Marian ran up to Amelia and seized her hand imploringly. "Please, don't leave us, Miss Wright!"

Shifting her gaze from Harrington, Amelia smiled down with genuine kindness at his little daughter.

"Don't worry, Marian. I'll be back." Turning back to him, she bobbed a slight curtsy. "Good day, my lord," she stated curtly. "I can tell when I am not welcome. I have obviously taken too much of your time, so I will be returning to Twickenham Manor."

He stepped closer towards her. Running his hand through his hair, he attempted again. "Please forgive my behavior, Miss Wright. I know you mean well. As for how I feel, it's difficult to explain."

"Don't bother." She turned to start walking on the dirt path that would eventually take her back to Aunt Nellie's.

"If you give me a moment, I will drive you home," he offered lamely.

"Not necessary," she called back, not bothering to turn around.

"It would only take a moment to hitch up the barouche!" he shouted at her retreating figure.

In response, she just held up her hand and waved.

Confounded woman! It was not proper for a female to walk unescorted. Did she have no consideration for her reputation?

Holding out his hand to his daughter, he said, "Let's get you back home quickly, my dear. It appears that I need to escort Miss Wright to Aunt Nellie's."

Innocently, Marian replied, "I don't believe she wants you to escort her anywhere, Father."

"She's just a confused young lady," he mumbled under his breath. Miss Wright was going to accept his assistance whether she wanted it or not. After all, he was a bloody gentleman!

Chapter 6

Marching across an expansive grass field, Amelia found herself growing angrier. How dare Lord Harrington treat her so rudely and so condescendingly! For heaven's sake, she was not the simple woman he thought her to be. She was a doctor! A doctor at Harvard Medical School. From an early age, she had set goals, and she had accomplished each one in due time. What had Lord Ninnyhammer accomplished? He was born into his title. He was not forced to earn what he had.

For Lord Harrington to treat her in such a rude, arrogant manner was a great insult. She was not a simple-minded woman that would be grateful just to be on the arm of a handsome man. She was a professional healer, for crying out loud! If ever a man needed healing, that one did!

Amelia's pace gradually slowed as the heat of the moment faded. Her eyes wandered over the vibrant green grass. Reviewing the confrontation with Lord Harrington in her mind, she was forced to admit that she did not belong in this era. She lived in a time when women had the same opportunities as men and were treated with equal respect. Well, maybe not always, but certainly more often than here! In 2018, there were female doctors and lawyers. Women even ran for president of the United States.

As fun as it was to dress in fancy gowns, it was not worth acting like someone she was not. Why had she thought she could just show up and insinuate herself into Lord Harrington's life? Perhaps it was time for her to recognize that some people were past the point of redemption. She felt a strong desire to go home and see her mother. Her steps faltered. Why was it so important to her mum that Amelia help Lord Harrington? In any case, it didn't matter. He would never accept anything from her.

Looking back at Belmont Manor in the distance, Amelia decided it was time to say goodbye.

A lone rider came up over the hill. Amelia immediately recognized the blue riding coat that was perfectly tailored to Lord Harrington's broad shoulders. He looked magnificent as his horse drew near, and she wished that things had turned out differently. However, she was finished arguing with this man, this so-called English "gentleman".

By the scowl on Lord Harrington's face, he was not pleased to see her, either. Without a word, he approached her, reined in his horse, and effortlessly dismounted. As he strode up to Amelia, he said, "Miss Wright, why…"

His scowl reignited her indignation. Fuming, the young American took a step closer to him, and he stopped speaking. "I will not mince words with you, Lord Harrington," she declared. She took another step, looking up at him. "Yes, I am opinionated and sarcastic. I apologize for that." Maintaining her gaze, she added, "But you have no right to speak to me as you have."

Lord Harrington shifted the reins in his hands, looking unsure of himself. "You ignore social etiquette, Miss Wright, and you are much too bold in your manner of speech."

"That is fair, but you, my lord, are rude and arrogant." She took a deep breath and began fidgeting with her bonnet strings. "Sometimes I see glimpses of a good, kind person, but then you become guarded, and I don't know what to make of you. Those two sides of you confuse and frustrate me. That fuels my own tendency to boldness. Again, I apologize."

He watched her silently, his eyes revealing nothing.

"I do wish you luck with Marian," she continued earnestly. "She is such a sweet, bright girl, but I think it's best that we part ways now." She lowered her hands and stood straighter. "Goodbye, Lord Harrington." She curtsied, silently praising herself for not losing her balance.

As she started to walk away, Amelia was pleased with herself. However, Harrington's next words caused her to stop in her tracks. "I seem to lose coherent thoughts around you!" he proclaimed. "And if I were honest with myself, I would admit that I am rather intimidated by you."

Turning around, she asked incredulously, "Intimidated? By me?"

"Yes," he answered, stepping closer to her. "You speak as freely as you laugh."

She smiled. "Did you just compliment me, or was that another thinly-disguised British insult?"

Chuckling, he replied, "It was a compliment." He took another step closer to her. "May I offer you another compliment?"

"By all means," she encouraged.

His blue eyes seemed to capture hers as he said, "I hope my daughter grows up to be a confident woman like you."

"I hope so, too," she murmured, knowing that Lady Marian would never be afforded the same opportunities that Amelia had. "In the place where I live, my lord, women are truly valued for their intellect."

A silence descended over them as they stared at each other, neither willing to make the first move to leave the field.

Finally, Amelia found the courage to inquire, "Do you recall a woman named Charlotte Wright?"

Lord Harrington's eyes sparked in recognition. "I haven't heard that name in almost eight years."

"Do you remember her?"

"I will never forget her," he whispered, almost reverently. "Are you a relation?"

"In a way," she answered, not willing to share her connection yet.

"I owe her my life." His words were filled with anguish.

With compassion in her heart, Amelia had an intense desire to put her arms around Lord Harrington to offer comfort, but knew she had no right to do so. Instead, she asked, "Will you share with me what happened?" She wanted to further understand her mother's connection to this enigmatic earl.

He shifted his gaze towards the horizon and didn't speak for a long time. Finally, he said, "After my wife died, I became inconsolable. To clear my mind, I used to walk to a large boulder that overlooked the River Thames and stare out into the water. The way the moonlight danced on the waves soothed me. How peacefully they moved and flowed! It was as though they could wash away my loneliness."

Amelia recalled the story her mother had told her of the day she'd met Adam Baxter, the Earl of Harrington. Mum hadn't been delusional after all!

"I was standing alone, knee-deep in the water, when a lovely woman dismounted her horse and entered the river beside me." His mouth twisted into a small smile. "Her dress was soaking up water, but she stood in the waves next to me for nigh onto an hour, almost as if she had the power to absorb a portion of my grief. We stood in silence until, at last, I came to myself and perceived that she was shivering with cold. I marveled that she made no complaint. When I helped her out of the water…" he paused, his voice hitching with emotions, "I felt… lighter, somehow."

Amelia thought about her mother and the gift of compassion that she shared so freely with others. "Lottie's greatest gift is her kind and loving nature."

"We met at that boulder every day for the next three weeks," Lord Harrington shared. "She gave me the strength to move on."

"Grief can be all-consuming, and sometimes it takes a friend to see you through," Amelia murmured softly.

Lord Harrington's watchful eyes were on her. "Are you and Lottie close?"

Amelia's emotions were stretched thin. All at once, it became too much for her, and her brave façade fell away. Unable to stifle her sob, she let the tears flow freely down her cheeks; tears that she had been holding in for months. "Yes! Lottie is *dying*, and all I can do is watch her suffer."

Harrington gently produced a monogrammed handkerchief for her to wipe her tears.

"I don't know what I am going to do when she dies. She is the last of my family. When she dies, I will be… *alone!*"

Not knowing what else to do, Amelia turned and walked swiftly away from him, toward Twickenham Manor.

"Wait!" Harrington called after her.

"I apologize, my lord. Please excuse me," she cried over her shoulder. Amelia hurried on, then stumbled over the uneven ground and her long skirts.

Dropping the reins, the earl ran after her. It took only a moment to overtake her, so he was able to catch her elbow before she fell. She took a few steps back, attempting to distance herself both emotionally and physically from him.

He started to step forward, then stopped. "I no more judge you for your tears than I judge myself for consoling you. You need not fear me."

To her surprise, he stepped forward and pulled her into a tight embrace. Almost of their own accord, her arms slid around him, and she buried her face upon the lapels of his coat.

As she allowed her head to remain on his chest, his heartbeat soothed her soul. Closing her eyes, she took in his smell of musk and leather, knowing this moment was fleeting. They were still from two different worlds, and nothing about their circumstances could change that.

When she was calmer, she stepped out of his arms and wiped her cheeks once more with his handkerchief.

"Thank you, Lord Harrington," she said, her eyes finally dried of tears. "I... I was wrong about you. You are a good man." She turned to walk away but was stopped by a gentle nudge on her shoulder. Peering over her shoulder, she was surprised to see the earl's horse following close behind her. The chestnut gelding nickered and nudged her softly again.

Amelia couldn't help but smile as she reached out to rub the horse's nose.

Harrington chuckled. "It seems Hamilton doesn't want you to walk alone." He reached for the reins, then bowed to her formally. "Miss Wright, will you do me the honor of allowing me to escort you home?"

Amelia hesitated. Then, tilting her head, she replied, "Yes, I will. Thank you, my lord."

And with those words, she felt something shift between them.

Sitting at his desk, Lord Harrington had spent all morning reviewing the ledgers, and he found he needed to rest his eyes and stretch his legs. A dozen chimes from the floor clock alerted him to the time. It was noon, and time for Aunt Nellie's picnic.

Miss Wright had invited him to attend the picnic when he'd escorted her back to Twickenham Manor, but as was his custom, he had declined. He hadn't been to a social gathering since his wife had died. He saw no reason to mingle with other gentlemen and simpering ladies, discussing the weather and avoiding any type of serious talk. No, he definitely did not want to go to that picnic.

However, an unbidden image of the impetuous young guest came to his mind. Harrington pictured her laughing at something another gentleman might say, her eyes twinkling intelligently. His hands subconsciously balled into fists. What if said gentlemen discovered what a truly remarkable woman she was? After all, it was only a matter of time.

Why did Harrington find Miss Wright so alluring? She defied convention, she mocked his title, and yet… he was drawn to her. Confounded woman! Why did she disrupt his thoughts in such an unrelenting fashion?

Making a quick decision, he shouted from his chair, "Blake!"

"Yes, milord," his butler replied, appearing quickly at the door to his study.

"Has an invitation recently arrived from Twickenham Manor?"

"Invitations arrive from Twickenham Manor on a weekly basis, but I dispose of them as per your instructions," Mr. Blake intoned, his stoic face giving nothing away.

"What are the invitations for?"

"Balls, soirees, social gatherings… events of that nature," Mr. Blake listed.

Harrington turned his head to look out the window. "Was I invited to a picnic today?"

Mr. Blake nodded. "Yes, on the east lawn."

Making his decision, the earl closed the ledger in front of him. "Have the groom ready my horse. I wish to attend."

"You wish to attend a *picnic*?" his butler asked with confusion in his voice.

"Yes, Blake." He rose from his seat and buttoned his coat. Moving around his desk, he was annoyed that his butler had not already left to do his bidding. "You are dismissed."

"As you wish, milord," Mr. Blake acknowledged before he slipped out of the room.

Stepping out into the hall, Harrington watched as his daughter ran down the stairs and headed straight towards him. "Is Miss Wright coming over today?" she asked breathlessly, stopping short in front of him.

"It is most unlikely, Marian."

She gave him a sad smile and looked down at her kid leather shoes. "I understand, Father."

Crouching down low, he met the child's gaze. "When I get home, would you like to play that game," he paused, searching for the words, "what did Miss Wright call it? Hide and go seek?"

She brightened at once and nodded energetically.

With a tender smile, the earl took a moment to look at his daughter. She had become such a lovely girl and looked just like her mother. "Perhaps I can persuade your delightful Miss Wright to join us."

A wide smile broke out on her face. "Do you promise?"

He chuckled, rising. "I cannot speak for Miss Wright, but I will make every effort to convince her to join us."

Reaching for his hand, Marian started leading him towards the door. "Off you go, Father. Off you go."

"Are you trying to get rid of me, you little imp?" he teased, relishing this moment with his daughter.

Marian gave him a sheepish smile. "The sooner you go see Miss Wright, the sooner you can convince her to come back."

As they arrived at the imposing front door, Blake extended his master's top hat and riding gloves, causing Harrington to release his daughter's hand. "Would you like an escort to join you, milord?"

"No, thank you, Blake, I am perfectly able to ride to Twickenham Manor alone," he assured, putting on his gloves.

Marian tugged at his green velvet coat. "Don't forget to be polite to Miss Wright."

He chuckled softly. "I will try."

A short ride later, Harrington came up over the small hill towards Twickenham Manor. The extravagant white estate was a beautiful backdrop for the large crowd milling about. Long tables were spread out along the east lawn, and shaded by colorful, striped tents. Servants were standing near the tables, ensuring there was enough food and drink for all.

A groomsman walked up to him and politely waited for him to dismount his horse. As soon as he handed off the horse, Aunt Nellie broke through the crowds to greet him.

"Lord Harrington," she exclaimed in a welcoming tone, "I am so happy to see you!"

"When did you start calling me Lord Harrington in private?" he teased. "Dear family friends don't make use of titles."

His gray-haired neighbor floated up to him and kissed his cheek. As she leaned back, her face held a warm smile, making him feel immediately at ease. "Adam, it has been entirely too long."

"Yes, it has, Aunt Nellie." Returning her smile, he was surprised at the lump in his throat. It felt divine to be welcomed in such a fashion.

Her eyes were filled with kindness. "How is Lady Marian?"

"She is well."

"You must bring her to Twickenham Manor for a visit."

"I will," he assured her, knowing that her invitation was in earnest.

Taking a fond look at his closest neighbor, Harrington was eternally surprised by Aunt Nellie's youthfulness. Even when he was younger, he never could get an accurate idea of how old she was, because she never seemed to age. She was a striking woman who had always showered him with an enormous amount of kindness and affection.

Aunt Nellie tucked her arm through his and led him towards the large crowd. "I truly am so pleased that you came to my intimate picnic."

"Intimate?" He chuckled. "My dear lady, this is a crush."

74

Pointing towards a long table, Aunt Nellie said, "If you are interested, my chef has prepared a delicious assortment of food. There is chicken pudding, and onion pie on that table." She pointed towards another table. "And that table has all types of delicious assortments of desserts, including your favorite, lavender cheesecake."

"Were you expecting me?" he jested.

"I knew you would come." Aunt Nellie gave him a secretive smile.

Before he could respond, his tall, broad-shouldered friend, Lord Wessex approached him with a gorgeous brunette woman on his arm. "Am I dreaming? Is my reclusive friend, Lord Harrington, actually attending a picnic?"

Adam smiled at his childhood chum. "After reviewing ledgers all morning, it seemed time for a much-needed distraction."

Lord Wessex tilted his head towards his companion. "Miss Peyton Turner, may I introduce you to Lord Harrington, who was my roommate at Eton and Oxford."

Amelia's fellow traveler removed her arm from Lord Wessex and curtsied. "Lord Harrington."

Harrington executed a bow. "Miss Turner." As he rose, he said, "You are American."

"I am."

He noticed her shoulders tighten and her jaw tense. Nevertheless, he pressed her, attempting to be subtle. "Did you arrive with Miss Wright?" Harrington knew very little about his daughter's favorite lady, and he realized he wanted to learn more about her.

Miss Turner shook her head, causing the thick brown curls that framed her face to swish back and forth. "No, she arrived earlier than I."

Curiosity won out, and he asked, "And when exactly did you arrive?"

"The night of the full moon, Lord Harrington," she replied, dismissively. "If you will excuse me, gentlemen."

As he watched Miss Turner walk swiftly away, her pale blue gown swaying back and forth, he was not prepared for his friend's annoyed question. "Why did you scare her off?"

"I did nothing of the sort, John," he defended. "Am I to understand that her Christian name is *Peyton*?"

"It is unusual, I will give you that." Wessex shrugged. "Perhaps it's a family name."

Lord Harrington scanned the crowd covertly, searching for Miss Wright. Where was she? He decided he needed to attempt to be social. "How did you come to be at this picnic, Wessex? Shouldn't you be out protecting English interests?" he asked, knowing that his friend worked for the home office.

Lord Wessex's blue eyes grew serious. "That is precisely what I am doing here." He stepped closer. "Two days ago, I was at a ball, and I met Miss Peyton Turner. When I heard she was American, I grew… interested."

"Do you take issue with her being an American?"

Wessex pursed his lips. "No, but I take issue if she is a spy for those colonial blackguards."

"Miss Turner does not look like a spy."

"That is precisely the point." He shifted his eyes back to the crowd. "Have you had a chance to meet her friend, Miss Amelia Wright?"

A surge of protectiveness welled up inside of his heart, baffling him. "I have, and I can confirm that she is not a spy."

"How can you be sure?"

Before he answered, Harrington saw Miss Wright suddenly separate herself from the clutch of picnickers, and she swiftly walked down a windy path towards the Thames. "When we first met, I thought she was applying for the position as my daughter's governess. She effectively informed me of my mistake," he revealed. He didn't bother to wait for a response as he turned to follow her.

Due to Amelia's purposeful stride, he found that he was a little out of breath when he found her. She was tucked into a cluster of birch trees, hidden from the prying eyes of the guests at the picnic. Her primrose gown billowed around her legs as she stared blankly out towards the river.

Not wanting to startle her, he spoke softly. "I beg your pardon, Miss Wright."

The lady whirled towards him, as if preparing for battle. When she saw him, she visibly relaxed. "Lord Harrington, how relieved I am to see you!"

Despite feeling pleasantly unsettled by her comment, he inquired, "What has upset you so?"

"Some of the men behind me were talking about how much they despise Americans. I understand their hostility towards my countrymen, I truly do, but I was not prepared for such vicious personal attacks."

Harrington was outraged. "I demand to know who said such horrific things to you!"

Walking over to a birch tree, she rested her back against the trunk. "Do not concern yourself. It was just a bit more than I had anticipated. The conversation centered around the subject of

American sailors being impressed to man British ships during these wars with Napoleon."

"It is Britain's right to search for deserters. Besides, it is the Americans that are wrong for employing our seamen when the Royal Navy needs them to man our warships."

Her hands grew animated while saying, "The Royal Navy may claim they are searching for deserters, but they impress Americans at their whim."

"And what say you about America attempting to trade with France illegally?" he asked, his voice becoming strained.

Amelia opened her mouth to speak, but closed it, looking reluctant to speak her mind, which was a first. "I do not care to express my opinion on the matter, my lord."

Being mindful of his previous conversation with his friend, Wessex, he cautiously pressed, "Miss Wright, forgive me, but I must ask. Are you an enemy of the Crown?"

Her eyes widened in surprise, and the color instantly drained from her face. "Of course not!" she answered fiercely, pushing away from the tree. "Some of the fondest memories of my youth are of my visits to England. In fact, my mother was born and raised here."

Harrington propped his boot on a tree stump and leaned forward till his arm rested on his knee. "For a woman, you seem to be remarkably informed about the American skirmish."

"Do I?" she laughed, fanning herself nervously.

As she started to walk past him, he dropped his foot and stood in front of her. "Are you in some kind of trouble, Miss Wright?"

She gave him a puzzled look, taking a step back. "Why would you ask me that… my lord?"

Instead of letting her retreat, the earl took a commanding step towards her. "Because if you are," he stopped, looking deep into her eyes, "I can help you."

Her gaze seemed to penetrate his very soul. "I thank you for your kind offer, but I am not in any trouble. That I know of," she amended hastily.

Harrington prided himself on being a gentleman, but he couldn't seem to stop himself from raising his hand and gently running his fingers across her lovely cheeks.

"My offer stands," he said softly.

Amelia closed her eyes and blushed at his touch, drawing his attention to her dark lashes as they fanned her face. When her eyes opened, he detected vulnerability in them.

"Why would you offer to help me?" she whispered, her voice barely audible.

He gave her a roguish smile. "Because…" He searched his feelings. He couldn't tell her the real reason, not yet. It was much too soon. Truth be told, he had no idea what his intentions were.

With great reluctance, the earl lowered his hand and stepped back. Despite showing incredible control over his impulses, he was still not ready to say goodbye to Miss Wright. "If you are not enjoying yourself at the picnic, perhaps you would be inclined to join Marian and me for a game of, what did you call it, 'hide and go seek' at my estate."

Relief was evident on her face as she smiled. "I would like that very much, thank you. Let me go tell Aunt Nellie."

Laura Beers

Chapter 7

"Thank you for the invitation to dine with you this evening," Amelia said, breaking the silence that had settled over the group. Lord Harrington sat at the head of the long table with Marian on his left and Amelia on his right.

Picking up his glass of wine, Lord Harrington took a sip before saying, "After your exertions entertaining my daughter this afternoon, it is our pleasure."

"This is the first time I have dined in this room!" Marian's excitement bubbled out and touched the hearts of both adults. "Father said it was a special occasion, so I'm to be on my best behavior."

Reaching for a fork, Amelia's hand stilled. "You don't eat dinner together as a family?"

After taking a bite of food, Lord Harrington swallowed before answering, "In England, children typically eat in the nursery, since they have not acquired the social etiquette to eat with the adults."

"I see," Amelia murmured, completely baffled by that logic. "And who teaches them the social etiquette that is required?"

Lord Harrington smiled at Marian. "A governess, of course." He shifted his gaze back to her. "Picking the right governess is of paramount importance. Not only is the governess responsible for implementing lessons during the day, with an emphasis on Latin and Greek, but they also teach them the social graces required."

As she reached for her glass, Amelia asked, "Then what is your role?"

"Generally, fathers do not take active roles in the lives of their children." Lord Harrington's tone was matter-of-fact as he wiped the corners of his mouth with a white linen napkin. "We have an estate to run."

"And the mother's role?" she pressed.

Lowering the linen napkin back to his lap, Lord Harrington's eyes turned sorrowful. "It depends. Some mothers rely solely on nannies and governesses to rear their children, but Marian's mother would have been actively involved with her, I'm sure."

Amelia turned her gaze towards Marian and saw her eyes staring at her plate, her expression sad. "Can you tell me about her?" she asked Lord Harrington.

He pressed his lips together. "Why would you want to hear about Agnes?"

"Because Agnes was Marian's mother, and I want to learn about the remarkable woman that she was," she admitted honestly.

"What exactly do you want to know?" His words were cautious.

Amelia gave him an encouraging smile. "How did you meet?"

"At a country dance," he answered wistfully. "She was the most beautiful woman in the room, and it took all my nerve to ask her to dance."

"Was it love at first sight?" she asked.

He nodded. "It was. Agnes was undoubtedly beautiful, but it was the way her eyes lit up when she smiled that beguiled me."

Amelia smiled as a footman came to clear her plate. "She sounds wonderful."

"She truly was." Lord Harrington's eyes grew reflective as he stared at his glass. "Agnes was kind-hearted and was constantly helping the people in the village."

"What a great legacy she left behind; not only was she a loving wife, but she loved serving other people," Amelia declared.

Sitting taller in her seat, Marian bobbed her head. "I want to be just like my mother when I grow up."

Lord Harrington reached over and patted his daughter's arm. "You are like her in so many ways. Your mother would be so proud to see the young woman you have become."

Marian beamed. "Truly, Father?"

"I am certain of it," he replied as he slid his arm back. He turned his gaze back towards Miss Wright. "Is rearing children so different in America?"

"I cannot speak for other families," Amelia hesitated, "but I was raised with both my parents being very active in my life."

"Did you have a governess?" Marian asked.

She shook her head. "No, but I did have a nanny when I was young."

"Were you sent away to boarding school, then?" Lord Harrington asked as a footman placed a dessert plate in front of him.

"I went to school during the day, but I came home in the afternoon," she said as a plate was placed in front of her, and she reached for her fork.

Lord Harrington gave her an understanding smile. "To further your lessons with a tutor?"

"Yes, in a way," she replied, returning his smile. "My father would give me mathematical equations to solve at his desk while he worked."

Harrington frowned, glancing at his daughter. "Was your father a professor?"

She took a bite of the pie and considered her next words carefully. "No, my father was a highly specialized doctor."

"What do you mean by 'a highly specialized doctor'?" Lord Harrington asked.

Amelia scrunched her nose. That was a misstep! "It means that he focused on conditions such as back pain, arthritis, and stiff muscles," she answered as vaguely as possible. "My father also performed surgeries to correct these issues."

"In England, physicians are regarded as gentlemen because of their schooling and lack of apprenticeship. Whereas, surgeons are considered more of a trade, because of their apprenticeship," Lord Harrington revealed. "Was your father a physician or a surgeon?"

"Both," she answered honestly.

Lord Harrington frowned. "I'm not sure why you would waste your time solving mathematical equations at your father's side. Don't you suppose that a better use of your time would be to focus on more ladylike pursuits?"

Rather than take offense, Amelia replied, "By ladylike pursuits, are you referring to embroidery, pianoforte, and making house calls?"

"Exactly." He smiled at her as he reached for his glass.

With a schooled expression, she stated, "I would much rather be with my father in the operating room than sipping tea and embroidering handkerchiefs."

Lord Harrington had just taken a sip of his drink and started choking at her remarks. A footman stepped up to see if he needed assistance, but he waved him off. After a moment, he turned his unrelenting stare at her.

"Tell me you are not in earnest, Miss Wright."

She shrugged. "But I am, my lord."

His eyes narrowed as he continued to watch her. "You are the most singular woman I have ever met."

"Thank you," Amelia responded, smiling.

"That was not meant as a compliment."

"I know," she answered, winking at Marian.

Lord Harrington huffed his disapproval. "I am of the belief that you need to be tutored in social etiquette."

She smirked, curious how this was going to play out. "Do you now?"

"Yes," he said. "Since you are helping me find a governess for my daughter, I would like to offer my humble services."

"To clarify," Amelia began, "you wish to tutor me on how to be a proper lady."

"Yes."

Amelia lifted her brow, feeling amused. "And how is it that you know so much about being a lady?"

Marian giggled as she continued to eat her dessert.

Lord Harrington took his linen napkin and tossed it onto the table. "That is precisely my point. A lady should always defer to a man."

Lifting her chin defiantly, Amelia stated, "I will defer to no man, Lord Harrington. After all, I am of the mindset that men and women are equal."

"That is American rhetoric," Lord Harrington proclaimed. "In England, men are responsible for the women under their care. Women cannot possibly understand the complexities that come with running an estate and must be sheltered from those burdens."

Amelia laughed dryly. "And what do you think of female doctors?"

"Women have delicate constitutions and would not be able to handle the vigorous workload of a physician. Furthermore, for a woman to display knowledge of the medical field is thoroughly unfeminine," he informed her. He pursed his lips before continuing, "However, I have met a few women that are decent midwives."

"And with that primeval comment, I think I should depart for the evening." Amelia rose from her seat, and a footman immediately stepped forward to pull the chair out.

Lord Harrington rose as well. "I thought this might be a good time to go over the stacks of correspondences for the position of Marian's governess."

Amelia glanced at the window and saw the sun was starting to set. "I should really be going back. I wouldn't want Aunt Nellie to worry."

"I will send over a missive to inform Aunt Nellie of your late departure," he said, offering his arm to her.

Marian placed her hand in hers. "Please stay, Miss Wright."

Knowing she was in a losing battle, Amelia placed her other hand on top of Lord Harrington's arm. "I will stay only because I want to find the best governess for Marian," she explained as she was escorted down the hall.

Once they entered Lord Harrington's study, Amelia removed her hand from his arm.

He retrieved a stack of papers from his desk and extended them towards her. "These are all the correspondences for the governess position."

Amelia accepted the papers and joined Marian on a settee in the corner. After they were situated, she started reading the beautifully-crafted letters while Marian leaned up against her.

"Why are you frowning?" Lord Harrington asked.

"Am I?" Amelia responded, looking up to see him sitting in a well-oiled, leather, wing-back chair behind his desk.

He grinned. "You are."

Lowering the papers to her lap, she replied, "Do you not intend to educate Lady Marian?"

"I have every intention of educating Marian, hence my need for a capable governess."

"No, you are a hiring a woman to..." Her voice trailed off as she picked up one of the letters and read, "help shape Lady Marian into a morally sound, docile, fashionable young woman ready to play by society's rules."

Lord Harrington crossed his arms. "I'm afraid I don't understand the issue."

"Interesting," she mumbled, lifting her brow in disbelief. "If I understand correctly, Marian's daily lessons will include learning Latin and Greek, the social graces required of her class, becoming competent in multiple musical instruments, practicing embroidery, and learning the skills to make a good match."

"That sounds accurate," Lord Harrington confirmed.

"What are the boys expected to learn?"

"Philosophy, logic, arithmetic, French, Italian, Latin, physics, and so on," he explained.

Looking at Marian, Amelia asked, "Do you not think it is important to teach your own daughter these subjects?"

"I have heard of some progressive parents teaching their daughters alongside their sons at home, but that would serve only as a disadvantage to Marian."

"And why would that be?"

Lord Harrington shifted his gaze towards his daughter. "Because if I did allow Marian to be well-educated, she would be forced to hide her intellectual prowess from the world or risk being shunned by society. Thus…"

"Thus, preventing her from obtaining an advantageous marriage," Amelia said, finishing his thought. Even though she thought it was an idiotic premise, she had no right to criticize their culture, especially since she was only visiting for a brief time.

"If I may be so bold," Lord Harrington began, "what attributes would you look for in a governess?"

A mischievous smile came to her lips. "I would want a governess that could fly."

Marian giggled. "No one can fly."

"Or perhaps a governess that could speak to animals?"

"Do be serious, Miss Wright," Lord Harrington contended.

Before she could reply, she heard a commotion coming from the main entry. Frowning at Harrington as she rose, she joined him to investigate the noise. She saw a group of maids huddled around Mr. Blake, and one had tears streaming down her face.

"What's wrong?" Amelia asked, approaching the crying maid.

The maid curtsied. "Nothing to concern yourself with, Miss."

"Nonsense," she replied. "How can I help you?"

With a trembling lip, the maid explained, "My sister's water broke yesterday shortly after sunrise, but the baby's head isn't down, and she is too exhausted to push the baby out."

Amelia's heart sank at those words. "Is a doctor with your sister?"

She shook her head. "No, Miss. Mrs. Watts, the midwife, is with her."

"Can you take me to her?" Amelia asked, knowing that she needed to act now or risk losing both the mother and the baby.

"I can. Do you think you will be able to help her?" the maid questioned between shaky breaths, nervously glancing over her shoulder.

Amelia followed the girl's gaze to see Lord Harrington standing in the hall watching them closely. His expression was stern, but she saw great compassion in his eyes. "I need your carriage at once, my lord," she demanded.

Harrington's next words were spoken with concern. "Miss Wright, it is best if you don't get involved. There is nothing you can do to help that poor woman."

"I have no doubt that I *can* help," she answered firmly. "I'm… a surgeon."

The coachman urged the team as fast as he dared through the darkening night, while Lord Harrington kept glancing at Amelia. She sat tensely on the bench beside him, holding onto the side of the carriage as they raced towards the village.

"Thank you, my lord. You didn't have to come."

"Nonsense, Miss Wright. It would never have done for me to allow my guest to go out into the night on an errand of mercy while I remained at home." The earl dismissed her comment with an impatient wave. As if to underscore his remark, loud sobs could be heard from the distraught young maid who hung on for dear life beside the driver.

The horses' hooves pounded on the deeply rutted dirt road, keeping time with Amelia's racing heart.

"If you please, turn down that road to the left," the young girl directed.

The coachman veered the carriage towards the road as the earl attempted to reason with Miss Wright again.

"This is ludicrous. Are you so cruel as to give this woman false hope?"

Amelia turned towards him with a determined gleam in her eye. "I do not expect you to understand, but I have the skills and mindset to save that woman."

He scoffed. "What are you going to do? Push the baby out yourself?"

"No, but there is another way."

"Women die from childbirth every day," he proclaimed crossly, eliciting another sob from the maid in the front. "That is just a fact."

"I don't have to accept that."

He ran his fingers through his hair. "Do tell me, Miss Wright, why are you so obstinate?"

"Because if I were not, who would enact change?" Amelia answered simply.

Harrington sat silently, having no answer for her.

He looked out the window and saw a small, stone cottage in the distance with smoke billowing up from the chimney. As they approached the home, a disheveled man burst outside, and his faded blue shirt hung out over his rough tan trousers. Recognizing this man as the village blacksmith, Henry Stevens, Harrington saw the pain on the man's face. Despite their difference in stations, it tore at his heartstrings.

The coach pulled up next to the blacksmith, who helped the maid step down. "Angela, bless ye for comin'," he said in a relieved tone.

Before Lord Harrington could come around to assist Miss Wright out of the carriage, she was already striding towards the cottage with Angela directly behind her.

The blacksmith approached his lord with eyes that were red-rimmed. "A thousand thanks, milord, for escortin' me sister-in-law all this way."

"It was my pleasure, Henry, but I should warn..."

Amelia stuck her head out the door. "Excuse me, sir, I need to speak to you about your wife."

Henry furrowed his brow and pointed over a shoulder with his outstretched thumb. "Who's th' lady, milord, and why did she just call me 'sir'?"

Harrington frowned. "A friend. Do as she says, Henry. She believes she can help your wife."

"All right, milord 'Arrington," Henry said, reluctantly moving towards the cottage door.

Ducking his head through the low doorway into the main room, the earl could see a small round stool in the corner by the crackling fireplace and a smoothly scrubbed table with benches in the center of the room. A side door was open, and he could hear moaning coming from within.

Amelia stepped into the main room as she wiped her hands with a cloth. "Mr. Stevens, is it?"

Henry stepped forward. "Yes, Miss."

Harrington was amazed to see that Amelia's demeanor spoke of confidence. With a strong, steady voice, she explained, "Angela told me your wife's water broke after sunrise yesterday. I have examined her, and your baby is breech. This has now become a medical emergency."

"Breech? Oh, law! Is my Amy goin' to die?" Henry cried, wringing his hands.

"Not if I can help it," Amelia asserted. "The baby's head isn't coming first. I can help Amy, but I need your permission to perform a procedure on her."

"A procedure?"

"It is a surgery called a cesarean section," she said. "I am going to cut your wife's belly open, remove the baby, and stitch her back up."

"Absolutely not!" Henry roared, but another long moan from his wife checked him. Her cries were weakening.

Expecting to see Amelia shrink back from Henry's adamant tone, Harrington was surprised to see her stand her ground. "I understand your reservations, Mr. Stevens, but your wife will die if I don't attempt this surgery."

Henry started pacing back and forth, tearing at his already wild hair. "Will she live if... you do this thing, Miss?"

"I cannot guarantee it, but I will do everything in my power to keep her alive," Amelia promised. "You need to know that this procedure will save the life of your baby. Without it, you will lose both of them."

Henry stopped and glared at her. "I ain't never heard of no female surgeon. 'Ow do I know ye can do this?"

"Where I am from, women are trained to do many things, including surgery," she explained, calmly. "Please, trust me. I can save Amy and your baby."

An older woman, with a cap covering her white hair, left the side room and approached Henry. "I believe her, Henry. This is the only way."

Pain was evident on Henry's brow as he implored, "How can you be so sure, Mrs. Watts?"

"Miss Wright has told us what she intends to do, and I believe it might prove successful," Mrs. Watts pressed. "But if we do nothing, your wife and baby will both die."

Henry turned his simple, pleading brown eyes to Lord Harrington. "What should I do, milord?"

Adam winced, loathe to make this mind-numbing decision for another man. His eyes went to Miss Wright, who was standing so brave and tall, but she was fooling herself. There was no way she could save Henry's wife from certain death. He would soon be mourning the loss of his wife and child.

As he opened his mouth to express his opinion, an unwelcome memory crashed into his mind.

The surgeon had just informed Harrington that nothing could be done to save his wife. After mumbling a pathetic apology, the surgeon left so he could say his final goodbyes to his wife. As he sat on the bed, he reached for Agnes's hand. Her skin had lost its glow, and

*her beautiful eyes were dull with exhaustion. "Adam,"
she whispered, "is the baby all right?"*

*"She is. A healthy baby girl," he replied as tears
welled in his eyes. "You did well, my love."*

*"I am... sorry... I won't," Agnes stopped,
attempting to catch her breath, "... be there... to watch
her grow up."*

*Tears rolled down his cheek. "Don't try to talk.
Just rest and try to get your strength back."*

*"You were my greatest joy," Agnes whispered
before her hand went limp in his desperate grasp.*

Never had he known such grief and torment after his
wife died. What would he have done if someone had given him
hope at that moment, even if it was only fleeting? The answer
was clear: he would have grasped it with both hands and pleaded
for more time with his wife.

Breaking his painful reverie, Harrington lifted his gaze,
his voice clear and unmistakable. "Henry, were I in your place, I
would do everything in my power to save my wife."

Henry bowed his head. "Then so be it." Turning towards
Amelia and Mrs. Watts, he pled, "Save my wife, Miss. Please,
dear God, *I can't lose her!*"

Amelia shot Harrington a grateful glance. "Thank you for
your vote of confidence, my lord." Turning towards Henry, she
stated, "Wait here, Mr. Stevens, and pray for your wife as you
have never prayed before. This may take a while."

Chapter 8

Striding purposefully into the side room, Amelia was back in her element. She had performed hundreds of c-sections as a third-year resident in obstetrics and had great confidence in her skill. Although, she had never done it by candlelight.

Accepting an apron from Mrs. Watts, she mumbled her thanks as she tied it around her waist. "Have you given her something for the pain?"

"Yes, I gave her laudanum this morning," Mrs. Watts replied.

The very first opioid drug, she thought. *Perfect.* "Give her a thimbleful while I drop the scalpel into the hot water."

Amelia walked over to a table and searched through Mrs. Watt's medical tools. Picking up the scalpel, she walked into the main room and placed it into the large pot that was hanging in the hearth. Taking time to carefully wash her hands, she then used a large spoon to carefully retrieve it from the bottom of the pot, knowing this was the best that she could do under the circumstances.

Looking around the room, she spotted Angela trembling in the corner. "Angela? Would you assist me, please?"

Eyes wide, the young maid followed Amelia into the room and stopped at the end of the bed. A sheet had already been placed under Amy in preparation for labor.

Pressing her hand to Amy's lower abdomen, Amelia informed Mrs. Watts, "I will need to stitch the abdomen and the uterus after I cut it open. Can you prepare the needle? Then, I'll need you and Angela to hold her legs and arms, so she doesn't flail when I cut her belly."

Pale, but following orders, Angela moved to the head of the bed, sitting beside Amy's head. She placed a wet cloth on her sister's forehead, then grabbed hold of her wrists, holding her arms still above her head.

Mrs. Watts laid the threaded needle on the nearby table, then moved to hold the laboring mother's legs.

Before she placed the scalpel to Amy's abdomen, Amelia asked, "Amy, can you hear me?"

Amy moved her head weakly. "Yes, Miss, but you are far away."

Knowing Amy was already under the influence of laudanum, she informed her, "I am about to make an incision, and it will hurt. Are you ready?"

"I am," she mumbled.

With a quick, smooth motion, Amelia sliced a horizontal incision about six inches long into her lower abdomen. Amy's loud scream filled the air, then all was silent as she passed out. Immediately, Amelia put her hands inside Amy, separating her abdominal muscles, finally making a horizontal cut into the lower section of her uterus.

Placing the scalpel on the bed, Amelia reached into Amy's abdomen and pulled out the baby. After gently handing the baby to Mrs. Watts, she cut the umbilical cord and was pleased to hear the baby's shrill cry fill the room.

"I have the baby, dear," Mrs. Watts assured her. "You finish with Amy."

Reaching back inside, Amelia ensured that the placenta was delivered properly before she started stitching up the uterus. Before closing the incision on the abdomen, she took her apron and tried to slow the blood flowing out. Taking great care, Amelia stitched up the new mother.

When she was finished, she moved tiredly to the water basin and washed her hands before she wet a linen cloth and started cleaning off the blood on Amy's belly. She watched as Mrs. Watts handed the swaddled infant to Angela. Amelia looked at the still-unconscious Amy, knowing she would probably not awaken until much later, perhaps not until morning.

After covering the new mother with a blanket, Amelia removed her apron and went to speak to Mr. Stevens. As she opened the door, both Lord Harrington and Mr. Stevens jumped up from their chairs. Their expectant expressions were nearly identical as they watched her face carefully. Smiling, she turned to Mr. Stevens. "Your wife and your baby girl are both doing well. Congratulations."

Mr. Stevens clapped his hands together as his wide grin showed pride and relief. "Amy is alive! Oh, saints be praised! Thank ye, Blessed Mother of God!" He danced a lopsided jig, then clapped a hand to his bearded face. "And I have a daughter!"

Putting her hand up to halt the giddy new father, Amelia explained in her no-nonsense doctor tone, "Amy is still sleeping and will be for several hours. Don't worry even if she sleeps until morning. I will be back tomorrow to follow up, but most likely I won't remove the stitches for fifteen days. As a precaution, Amy is not allowed to leave her bed for the first three days. Angela can see to her private needs until then."

Lord Harrington cleared his throat, clearly uncomfortable with the subject at hand.

Ignoring him, she added, "If you do not follow my directions precisely, there is a chance that the stitches will rupture, or infection could set in, and your wife will die."

Mr. Stevens nodded slowly, but his smile never dimmed. "I understand, Miss."

"Good." She turned to Lord Harrington. "My lord, will you ensure that plenty of fresh vegetables, leafy greens, fruit, and meat are delivered here as quickly as possible? Amy needs plenty of food, since she is now caring for a baby, as well as herself."

Bemused, Harrington simply nodded.

A smile played on Amelia's lips as she saw Mr. Stevens practically dancing in a circle as he kept glancing at the door separating him from his wife and child. "You are welcome to go see them."

Amelia had barely finished her sentence when the burly man ran past her. Turning back towards Lord Harrington, she was surprised to see he was staring at her once-pristine gown. Glancing down, she saw that it was covered with blood.

Lord Harrington took a step closer, reaching towards her with deep concern. "Were you injured during the surgery, Miss Wright?"

"This is not my blood," she assured him. "It is all from Amy."

Slowly, he swiped his chin with his hand, looking a bit worse for wear himself. "That is a great deal of blood."

Walking over to the water basin near the fireplace, Amelia scrubbed the stains from her arms and hands, especially under her nails. "Heavy blood loss is common during a cesarean delivery," she explained.

"And Mrs. Stevens survived?"

"She was magnificent."

"Miss Wright, how did you…" His words trailed off as he shook his head slowly, trying to understand.

Using a relatively clean, dry cloth that hung near the basin, the young doctor dried off her arms. "How did I what, my lord?"

"How did you… *know*… what to do?"

Amelia smiled, taking pity on the handsome earl. "I told you, I am a surgeon."

"That is impossible," he huffed. "I've never heard of a female surgeon."

Feeling no need to argue, she stated, "Regardless, Amy is alive, as is her baby."

"I can't believe you saved them both," Lord Harrington said with awe in his voice. "What you did here in this simple hut was nothing short of a miracle."

"Birth is always a miracle, my lord," she contended softly. "I did what I was trained to do. That is all."

Mrs. Watts emerged from the bedroom with a bright smile on her face. "Well done, Miss Wright! Wait until the other midwives hear about this…"

Amelia cut her off. "You mustn't tell anyone," she said urgently. "Promise me that you won't discuss what was done here."

"But why, dear?" Mrs. Watts asked. "You should be praised for what you did for the Stevens family."

"I did not ask for praise. I only did what needed to be done," she insisted. "Please, promise me."

"On my honor, I won't tell a soul," Mrs. Watts said, eyeing her with concern. "However, Bexmore is a small village. I have no doubt that the news will travel fast."

Shifting her gaze towards Lord Harrington, Amelia asked, "Are you ready to depart, my lord?"

"Yes," he answered with a puzzled expression, "if you are, Miss Wright."

As she walked out of the cottage, Amelia felt a sense of dread wash over her. Would Aunt Nellie be furious that she had performed a c-section? After all, according to her medical books, the first known instance of a British surgeon performing the surgery with both mother and child surviving was in 1826.

Her steps faltered. Did her actions just alter the course of history?

She allowed Lord Harrington to assist her into the carriage. "Thank you," she murmured.

As the coachman guided the horses back towards Belmont Manor, Harrington gave Amelia only side-long glances. She was relieved that he didn't attempt to start a conversation with her, and simply stared out into the darkness in silence. Emotionally, she was exhausted, and she was trying to imagine what Aunt Nellie would do when she told her what had transpired at the cottage. What if Aunt Nellie zapped her with her magic, and she was forced to live the rest of her life as a bug?

Harrington's voice broke into her thoughts. "I know I did not express myself adequately back there, but I am impressed that you saved Mrs. Stevens and her child."

"Thank you, Lord Harrington," she said, giving him a tentative smile.

Leaning back, he put his right arm on the back of the bench, shifting his body towards her. "How did you learn to perform a…"

"Cesarean delivery."

"I am unfamiliar with that term," he admitted with a chuckle. "Did you assist your father with these types of surgeries?"

She wanted to say, no, I went to medical school, and I am a doctor in the year 2018. Instead, she replied, "I have trained with the best."

Lord Harrington smiled sadly. "I wish that you'd been here to save my Agnes."

"Forgive me if I'm intruding, but what were the circumstances of her death?"

Removing his arm from behind Amelia, he clasped his hands tightly together. "The same as Mrs. Stevens. Marian's head didn't come first." His words were so quiet that Amelia almost didn't hear him.

"Did Agnes get to see Marian before she died?"

He shook his head. "After the delivery, Agnes was too exhausted to even keep her eyes open."

Amelia gently placed her hand on the sleeve of his riding coat. As he brought his gaze up to meet hers, she hoped that her next words would convey the depths of her sympathies for him. "I am so sorry for your loss. It sounds like Agnes was an incredible woman."

His eyes crinkled at the corners as sadness marred his features. "I believe you could have saved her," he said, his voice hitching with emotion.

It was the last thing spoken between them as they drove back to Twickenham Manor.

The following morning, Amelia placed her hand on the door handle, debating about just turning around and running far, far away. She had tossed and turned all night in bed as she thought about Aunt Nellie's possible reproach.

Perhaps she could just write a letter and slip it under the door. She sighed. When did she grow so spineless? Oh well, this conversation had to happen, she knew. Taking a deep breath to gather her courage, she pushed open Aunt Nellie's study door.

"Good morning, Aunt Nellie," she said with far too much effort.

Aunt Nellie lowered the paper that she was reading and gestured to a chair. "Please sit, Amelia. We haven't had a chance to discuss your evening with Lord Harrington. Marie mentioned the dress that you were wearing last night was ruined," Aunt Nellie stated as she leaned back in her chair, her expression giving nothing away. "Would you mind explaining how so much blood got onto a very expensive gown?"

Gnawing her bottom lip, Amelia ventured, "I may have broken the space-time continuum."

Putting her elbows onto her desk, Aunt Nellie rested her chin in her hands. "Oh, dear. I think you'd better start at the beginning. This sounds like a fantastical story."

Attempting to buy herself some additional time, Amelia smoothed out her pale blue day dress. "After the picnic, Lord Harrington escorted me to his estate, and we played games with his lovely daughter, Marian." Her eyes roamed the room as she took in all the shelving that contained piles and piles of books.

"After playing on the lawn, we had a delicious dinner. We discussed…"

Aunt Nellie started laughing. "Good heavens, child. You are babbling. Get to the point, if you please!"

Squeezing her eyes shut, Amelia admitted, "I performed a cesarean delivery on a woman in the village."

"Did you now?"

Amelia clasped her hands tightly in her lap and scrutinized her white knuckles. "Yes, Aunt Nellie, I cut the baby out of the woman's stomach because she was unable to deliver it on her own."

"Oh my!" Aunt Nellie exclaimed, dropping her hands into her lap. "Did the woman live?"

"Yes."

"And the child?"

"She lived as well."

Aunt Nellie lifted her brow. "Then, what is the problem?"

She lowered her gaze as she admitted, "I performed a procedure that is not medically recognized in this era."

"Does this procedure cause heavy blood loss?"

"It does."

Aunt Nellie slapped her hand onto the desk. "That explains how your dress was ruined." She smiled. "I told Marie that you were not slaughtering cattle."

"Why would I slaughter cattle?" she asked in confusion.

"We just couldn't figure out how all that blood got onto your dress." Aunt Nellie shrugged and rose, changing the subject. "What would you think of joining Miss Turner and me? We are going to London to get some lemon ice from Gunter's. I know it is almost a two-hour drive by carriage, but I keep hearing how delicious it is.

Amelia gaped openly. "Aren't you upset with me?"

Aunt Nellie came around her desk and sat down on the chair next to her. "Quite the opposite, in fact. I am proud that you saved that woman from death."

"But didn't I just destroy the very fabric of time?"

Chuckling, Aunt Nellie gave her a head shake. "It doesn't work that way. As I shared before, time is a fuzzball," she explained. "Every person has their own thread of time, and there is no space-time continuum."

Amelia sighed in relief. "I was afraid that you were going to turn me into a mouse."

"A mouse?"

She nodded. "Or a roach."

"Why would I turn you into a rodent or a bug?" Aunt Nellie asked, eyeing her with disbelief.

"It seemed logical to me," she said, feeling relieved at the tone of this conversation.

"You have the most vivid imagination." Leaning forward, Aunt Nellie patted her knee as she asked, "Now, how are things progressing with Lord Harrington?"

Amelia smiled. "Things are going well. He is spending more time with his daughter and seems to be much happier than when I first saw him."

"Excellent news," Aunt Nellie confirmed. "Have you found a governess for Marian?"

"Not yet," the younger woman admitted. "We were interrupted last night."

"I understand. I'm sure everything will work itself out in due course. By the way, you will be pleased to know that I secured invitations for us to attend the Duke of Albany's ball in four days," Aunt Nellie revealed, beaming with excitement.

Amelia stifled a groan. "To be honest, I am tired of the thinly veiled insults about my American heritage." She tossed up her arms. "I get it," she stated dramatically. "I am an American, and we are at war with Britain. But *I* didn't start that war, and I'm not a spy trying to discover British war secrets."

With a mischievous smile, Aunt Nellie said, "Just leave the specifics up to me."

Catching her hostess's mood, Amelia grinned and nodded. "Yes, ma'am."

"Now, I don't believe you answered me about visiting Gunter's tea shop for some lemon ice," Aunt Nellie said, rising from her seat. "Let's shop for some ribbons as well."

"Sounds perfect," Amelia agreed. "I'll go find Peyton."

Laura Beers

Chapter 9

"Blake!" Lord Harrington roared from his chair in his study. "Get in here."

Mr. Blake appeared from the hall and bowed. "Yes, milord."

"Where are the notes from the tenants' meeting?"

Giving him a curt nod, his butler slipped his hands into his pocket and pulled out a few sheets of paper. "They were just delivered."

Accepting the papers, he grumbled, "Next time, I want these notes sooner."

"As you wish, milord," Blake replied. "May I get you anything else?"

The earl waved his hand, dismissing his servant. He didn't have time for such incompetence. He had an estate to run, tenants to be cared for, and his presence was requested at the House of Lords for a special vote this evening.

Reaching into the pocket of his ivory brocade waistcoat, he removed the note that Miss Wright had written to him and slipped under his study door earlier. Despite her riding over to his estate to visit Marian, he hadn't had any time to spend with the remarkable young female surgeon. He grimaced, knowing that was not entirely true. He was avoiding her. To make matters worse, he didn't fully understand why.

Unfolding the note, Adam shook his head fondly at Miss Wright's straightforward and uncomplicated letter-writing style.

Lord Harrington,

I hope all is well. I have missed spending time with you.

-Amelia

Without thinking, he ran his fingers over her name. Did she now grant him leave to call her by her Christian name? After all, Miss Wright did not seem to care about breaking social customs. Why did the memory of her inflict turmoil in his heart and soul? He couldn't explain why he was drawn to her to such a degree.

"What do you have there?" a familiar tenor voice interrupted Harrington's reverie.

Folding the note, Harrington quickly placed it back into his waistcoat pocket before acknowledging the irritation before him. "How the blazes did you get past Blake, Wessex?" he grunted.

"Blake did announce me, but you were too preoccupied with that note to notice. Was that from Miss Amelia Wright?"

"It is none of your concern," he declared, rising from his seat.

"Tut, tut, Harrington." Lord Wessex straightened up from the desk with an annoying glimmer of a grin on his face. "I didn't realize that you two had grown so close these past few days."

"Leave it alone, John." The earl stepped over to his drink tray and pulled the top off of the decanter. After he poured port into two glasses, he handed one to his friend.

Accepting the glass, Wessex just watched him, and Harrington found the scrutiny disconcerting. "Do you care to comment on why I just saw Miss Wright playing with Marian on the lawn?"

"Is she?" Harrington asked before he took a sip of his drink. "I hadn't noticed."

"They were chasing each other across the lawn, playing a game of… 'tag', I believe."

"It is an American game, I presume," Harrington replied nonchalantly.

"Why is Miss Wright spending time at your estate?" his friend asked as he swirled his drink in his hand.

"It is none of your business." Harrington gulped down his port.

"It is," Wessex insisted, lifting his brow, "if she is a spy."

Adam slammed his glass down on the tray. "Stop being so thick-headed, Wessex!"

"Just hear me out," his friend protested, holding up his left hand. "I have deduced that Miss Turner and Miss Wright have no reason whatsoever to be in England. *Two* lovely, intelligent American ladies appear out of the blue sky." Wessex placed his glass down on the tray. "How they arrived is shrouded in secrecy, but we both know that they could not have traveled here on an American or British ship."

"Even if what you are saying is true," Adam glowered, "what makes you think these two ladies are acting as spies?"

"Perhaps their job is to befriend lords and high-ranking officials in hopes of stealing secrets," Wessex speculated.

"No," Harrington insisted. "I can vouch for Miss Wright with certainty. She is no spy."

"You are blinded by her feminine wiles," Wessex accused.

"Tread lightly, my friend. Choose your words with care."

His friend sat on a nearby chair before probing, "Then explain to me what happened with Miss Wright at Mr. Stevens' house?"

Realization dawned on him as he stared at his companion. "Have you been spying on me?"

Lord Wessex shook his head. "No. However, we have been watching Miss Wright's movements, and your paths appear to cross often."

Tilting his head back, Harrington looked up at the rafters before saying, "Miss Wright performed a cesarean delivery on Mrs. Stevens, the blacksmith's wife in the village."

"A Cesarean delivery? What in blazes is that?"

Harrington sighed. "It's a procedure to remove the baby from the womb to preserve the baby and the mother."

Wessex frowned.

"Mrs. Stevens would have died if Miss Wright hadn't performed the procedure to save her and the baby."

Wessex perched on the edge of his seat, leaning toward his friend. "How did she learn how to do that?"

He shrugged. "She claims she's a surgeon."

"A surgeon?" Lord Wessex repeated incredulously. "I find that highly unlikely. Women can't be surgeons, even American women. Their constitutions are much too delicate."

"I am just telling you what she said and what I saw," Harrington retorted. "Miss Wright was magnificent." He paused, recalling the moment accurately. "She did not hesitate to run to Mrs. Stevens' aid, nor did she faint or squirm at the sight of blood. She performed the office as competently as any man I have ever seen. I tell you, Wessex, she was a triumph!" His words stilled when he saw Wessex's obnoxious grin. "Why are you smiling like a bloody fool?"

"You find her handsome, don't you?" Wessex asked.

"Yes, of course. What man wouldn't?"

"But her behavior, her manner of speaking is… unconventional, wouldn't you say, Harrington?"

"Yes, there is no denying that. What of it, Wessex?"

"Then, are you in love with her, or are you just… toying with her emotions?"

"What! No… you are speaking rubbish," Harrington sputtered.

"You love Miss Wright," Wessex asserted.

Harrington raked his hand through his brown hair. "I barely know her. That is impossible."

"Is it?" Wessex persisted. "If I recall, you fell in love with Agnes in a similar fashion."

"No, no, no…" he stammered out. "Agnes is my wife, and I love her."

Harrington's oldest friend rose from his seat, his eyes reflecting pity. "No. Agnes *was* your wife, and you will always love her. But Agnes was my friend as well, and she wouldn't have wanted you to remain alone. She wouldn't have wanted Marian to be without a mother."

"I don't have time to search for another wife," Harrington mumbled, but his heart wasn't in it.

Stepping to the window, John looked out over the lawn. "Fortunately, you don't have to search very hard… assuming she is not a spy."

"She is not a spy," Harrington growled.

"Then help me prove it." Wessex turned back around. "Arrange a meeting with Miss Wright and allow me to ask her a few questions."

"I can do that…" His words stopped when Marian ran into the room with her arms wide open. Crouching down, he opened his arms as his daughter flew into them. "Miss Wright left for the day," she informed him.

"Did she?"

"Yes." Marian nodded. "And I came and told you straightaway, just as you instructed me to do."

Ignoring his friend's chuckle, Harrington pressed, "What did you two discuss?"

Marian pressed her lips together just as he had seen Amelia do in the past. "We discussed my lessons, and I played a song for her on the pianoforte."

"Anything else?"

Nodding her head, his daughter whispered loudly, "Miss Wright was excited to go to a ball tonight."

"A ball?" he asked in surprise. "Whose ball?"

"She didn't say, Father."

He frowned. He was not pleased with this turn of events.

Wessex chuckled from behind him. "Most likely, it is Albany's ball."

Turning his head towards his friend, he asked, "Were you invited?"

"I was, in fact."

The earl rose from his crouched position, attempting to keep his face expressionless. "Perhaps we should stop by the ball after the vote at the House of Lords tonight."

Lord Wessex's smile grew as he asked, "Are you going to cite a reason other than going to spy on Miss Wright?"

"I… haven't been to a ball in ages," Harrington attempted dryly. "Miss Wright's attendance is merely an added bonus."

"You're making yourself a fool," Wessex warned.

"Blake!" Harrington shouted, leaving his study. "Is my blasted coach ready?"

He shook his head as he listened to his daughter giggling and Lord Wessex roar with laughter. Was he, indeed, making himself a bloody fool?

Dressed in a beautiful gown with roses embroidered along the square neckline, Amelia watched out the carriage window as they approached the townhouse belonging to the Duke of Albany. At the top of the long drive was a massive estate with white columns framing the exterior of the home. "This is considered a *townhouse*?"

"This is the duke and duchess' primary residence, but they do spend time at their country homes during the fall and winter months," Aunt Nellie informed them.

"Where I live, a townhouse is *very* different," Amelia remarked, keeping her eyes on the line of carriages still waiting to be unloaded.

Peyton laughed as she ran her hands down her silver gown. "We should just move into that townhouse. After all, I doubt the duke would even know we were there."

"Now, girls," Nellie said, drawing back their attention, "I have a wonderful surprise for you."

After a long, drawn-out moment, it became clear that Aunt Nellie wasn't going to say anything more, so Amelia asked, "Can you tell us what it is?"

"You will see," Aunt Nellie replied with a secretive smile.

The carriage jerked to a stop, and a footman opened the door, extending his hand towards them. Amelia placed her gloved hand into his and stepped down onto a stone pathway that led up to the largest set of red doors that she had ever seen.

As she approached the entry, two uniformed footmen pushed open the red doors, and she walked into a magical ballroom. There was something to be said for stepping back into such an elegant era. The large rectangular room was lit with hundreds of flickering candles set in ornate chandeliers hanging low from the ceiling. Gold paper lined the walls, and a beautifully chalked mural was drawn onto the center of the dance floor.

Despite being hated because of her American heritage, Amelia did not seem to mind being there as much as she thought she would. To be in this ballroom was a moment she knew she would treasure. She took a step forward towards the crowd but was stopped by Aunt Nellie's hand on her arm.

"First, I must introduce you to someone," she instructed, leading her and Peyton towards a small hall off the ballroom.

Once Aunt Nellie arrived at the door, she knocked and pushed it open. They were greeted by the sight of a lovely older woman with faded brown hair, dressed in a mauve-colored gown and draped with jewels, including a large tiara crowning her head.

Once the door was closed behind them, the woman directed her next question towards Aunt Nellie. "Are these the girls you were telling me about?"

"They are," Aunt Nellie answered. "Your Grace, the Duchess of Albany, may I present Miss Peyton Turner and Miss Amelia Wright?"

"Your Grace," they both murmured in unison, dipping into low curtsies.

The duchess rose and walked closer to inspect them, her eyes roaming their faces and clothing. In one hand, she held a fan that she tapped into the palm of her other hand.

"Aunt Nellie, they are exquisite."

"Do you think you can help them?" Aunt Nellie asked.

"Of course," the duchess said, flipping open her fan. "We time travelers must stick together."

Amelia gasped. "*You* are a time traveler?"

The duchess sat down gracefully. "Please, sit down, and we can have a quick chat before we go out and meet your adoring fans."

"The English hate us," Peyton sighed as she sat on an upholstered armchair.

Nodding, the duchess responded, "They don't hate *you*, but they do hate Americans and everything that the American people believe in."

Peyton giggled. "Thank you for that clarification."

Smiling, the duchess revealed, "I originally traveled from the year 1998 back to 1783. I visited Twickenham Manor while I was participating in a study abroad program at Arizona State University. I was a history major, in fact." With a nod towards Aunt Nellie, she continued, "I decided to go exploring one night when the moon was full."

"On the fourth floor?" Amelia guessed.

The duchess nodded.

"Did you experience any effects from time travel?" Peyton asked.

"I did," the duchess confirmed. "My teeth chattered for almost an hour afterwards."

"My ears started ringing," Amelia confessed.

Peyton placed a hand to her stomach. "I was nauseous."

Amelia frowned. "If you were sent to the year 1783, why did you not travel back during the next full moon?"

"Because of me," a deep, male voice said, as he entered through a side partition. "I convinced her to stay and marry me."

As they started to rise, the barrel-chested duke put his hand out to stop them. "Please, stay seated." Striding over to his wife, he joined her on the settee. "My wife informed me of your precarious situation, and we want to help you."

"How can you help us?" Peyton asked.

The duchess had a twinkle in her eyes. "It is quite simple. You are our dear friends from America, and we invited you to England for the Season."

"But that does not explain how we arrived," Amelia pointed out.

The Duke of Albany laughed. "Oh, my dear, innocent child. Once we endorse you, no one will harass you again, or I will ensure they are given the cut direct."

Peyton whispered to Aunt Nellie, "Does that work?"

"It does," the duchess answered for her. "Trust us. You will have a wonderful Regency Immersion Experience, I can promise you that."

"Perhaps you will fall in love," the duke said, winking impertinently, "and decide to stay."

Both women protested vigorously before Peyton explained, "I am an English teacher back home."

"I'm an obstetrician," Amelia added. At the duke's puzzled expression, she clarified, "A doctor for childbearing women."

The duke lifted his brow. "A female doctor. What's next, a female barrister?"

"Ignore my husband, my dears. I do all the time," she teased, swatting playfully at her husband.

Amelia bit her lower lip as she debated asking her question. Finally, finding the nerve, she asked the duchess, "Your Grace, why would you give up all that you had, and all of your comforts, to stay in this time?"

The duchess's face softened as she looked lovingly over at her husband. "To me, I gave up nothing and gained everything."

Leaning over, the aging duke kissed his wife, whispering something in her ear that caused her cheeks to turn pink. Standing up, the duke pulled down his red, paisley waistcoat and asked the group, "Shall we?"

The duchess reached for her husband's arm. "You must plan to call on us before you return home on the next full moon. I am curious what happens in the future."

Walking into the ballroom, the Duke and Duchess of Albany were announced, and the whole room grew silent as they entered. She was surprised when the duke and duchess stopped in the center of the room and turned back towards them, smiling.

The duchess leaned over to kiss her cheek, and whispered, "Smile. Remember, we are dear friends." After the duchess kissed Peyton's cheek, she assured them, "Go enjoy yourselves. You will find the patrons in this room will be much more accommodating towards you."

As the duke and duchess glided off, Aunt Nellie stood next to them and looked at each in turn. "Are you girls prepared to be the belles of the ball?"

Without warning, gentlemen swarmed around them like bees to honey, requesting dances. With a gleam in her eye, Amelia whispered to Peyton, "What a pleasant change."

An Unexpected Gentleman

Chapter 10

"Blazes," Lord Harrington mumbled as he brought the flute of champagne to his lips.

Lord Wessex chuckled next to him. "Miss Wright and Miss Turner don't seem to lack for dance partners this evening."

An unfamiliar surge of jealousy washed over him as he watched Miss Wright danced the quadrille. He wondered why she was smiling at her partner. For the past hour, he had observed gentlemen leading her out to the dance floor, and he was becoming progressively more agitated as the night wore on.

"You are grinding your teeth," Wessex informed him.

Harrington tossed back the remainder of his drink and placed the flute onto the tray of a servant passing by. "I don't know what bloody well happened," he grumbled. "When did she become so well received by the ton?"

"If you aren't in love with her, then why are you so jealous?"

"I most certainly am not in love…" He stopped speaking as he recognized the music for the quadrille was beginning to wind down. Immediately, he started striding towards Amelia, ignoring the anger building up when he saw her partner lead her off the dance floor.

Stopping at the edge of the crowd, he watched Miss Wright approach. She was dressed in a rose gown that showed her figure to perfection. Her brown hair was piled high on her head, with satin ribbons woven throughout, drawing his attention to the long, elegant curvature of her neck. Good gracious, she's beautiful, he thought.

Then, the realization hit him. He *was* in love with Miss Wright. How was that possible? He didn't have time to pursue that line of thought, however. All thoughts disappeared when he saw the lady notice him for the first time. Her eyes lit up, reflecting happiness, as she dropped her partner's arm and moved towards him.

Not acknowledging any other gentlemen, she stopped in front of him with a hopeful smile on her face. "I have missed you, Lord Harrington."

He smiled broadly. "I have missed you as well, Miss Wright."

"Where have you been?"

Mindful of prying eyes, he offered his arm while asking, "Would you care to dance?"

She curtsied. "I would be honored, my lord."

When Amelia placed her gloved hand onto his arm, Harrington felt alive, as if a frisson had passed through him. Feigning indifference, he led her out to the dance floor. Once they stopped, he heard the first strains of the waltz. Feeling her tremble at the touch of his hand on her back, he was touched by the trust in her face as she smiled up at him. He found that she molded perfectly into his arms, and he suddenly had no intention of ever letting her go.

"Are you enjoying the ball, Miss Wright?" he asked politely.

Her fingers tightened around his shoulder. "I am. It is all so unreal," she breathed. "I am dancing the waltz in a duke's ballroom."

Pulling her closer, he said, "The vote in Parliament took longer than anticipated, and I rushed over thinking you would be a wallflower."

As their arms rose during the dance, their faces were mere inches from each other, and he was rewarded to see a blush on Amelia's cheeks. She lowered her gaze before sharing, "The Duke and Duchess of Albany have endorsed us. Miss Turner and me, I mean."

"Did they now?"

She brought her beautiful green eyes up, and he admired the yellow flecks in them. "They did. Which is why we have been inundated with dance partners."

Adam gave her an impish grin. "I believe there is another reason."

"You do?" she asked with a puckering of her brow.

He waited till they lifted their arms again, before revealing, "The ton has finally recognized what a remarkable woman you are."

She smiled coyly. "Careful, my lord, it almost sounds as if you are flirting with me."

Leaning closer, he whispered next to her ear, "I believe you are correct, Miss Wright."

"In that case, I would prefer that you address me by my given name," she said lightly, eyebrows raised.

Harrington straightened and smiled. "Amelia, then. And I would rather you call me Adam."

"Adam," she repeated. "I find that name has a considerably better ring to it than Lord Ninnyhammer."

"I agree."

Their steps slowed as the music came to an end, but Adam was not ready to relinquish Amelia just yet. "Would you mind terribly if we took a walk on the veranda?"

She beamed up at him. "Not at all."

He offered his arm, and she accepted it. "I apologize for being so busy these past few days, Amelia."

"Marian has missed you," she murmured.

"Just Marian?"

Amelia barely nudged him with her shoulder, a treat that he found delightful. "I believe I already admitted that I have."

Leading her onto the veranda, Adam found a quiet corner, tucked away from the light of the ballroom. He stopped in front of an iron railing and dropped his arm, shifting towards her. "You look lovely tonight, Amelia."

She lowered her gaze, but even the dark night could not hide her flushed cheeks. It appeared that she wasn't completely immune to his charms. This boded well for him.

Amelia regarded him with curious wonder, drinking in the features of his face. "You seem different tonight, Adam."

"I'm starting to see clearly for the first time in ages," he revealed, locking his gaze with hers.

"Oh? What do you see clearly?" she asked demurely, her eyes dropping to his lips.

He cleared his throat, wishing they were somewhere more private. "I believe I am ready to start courting again."

Amelia stared back at him, blinking rapidly, and he detected vulnerability in her eyes. After a long pause had passed between them, she gave him a tight smile. "That's great news," she exclaimed in what seemed to be an insincerely cheerful voice.

"Is it?" he replied suddenly suspicious.

Placing her hand on his sleeve, Amelia nodded. "Yes, I think it is brilliant. You need a wife, and Marian needs a mother."

Adam pressed his lips together, puzzled at her attitude. "Precisely what I was thinking."

"Why didn't I think of this?" she declared, withdrawing her hand. "A wife will make you happy."

He attempted to reach for her right hand so he could declare his intentions, but Amelia stepped away from him. Not only did she seem oblivious to his attempt, but she started pacing back and forth. "What attributes are you looking for in a suitable wife?" she asked.

"Attributes?" He wondered what in the blazes she was talking about.

She stopped pacing and asked, "Do you want a witty wife, or do you prefer a more docile woman?"

Adam closed his eyes in mortification. Amelia thought she was going to help him find a wife. What she failed to recognize was that he already had chosen *her* to be his wife. Turning his back to her, he put his hands on the iron railing and sighed, slumping his shoulders. Their conversation had begun so well. How had it so quickly turned sour?

While Adam was mustering up the courage to try again, he heard Lord Wessex say, "Pardon the interruption. I was hoping for an introduction to the lovely Miss Wright."

Turning back around, he quickly made the introductions. "Miss Amelia Wright, may I introduce my childhood friend, Lord Jonathan Wessex?"

Wessex reached for her hand, bringing it up to his lips. "I am delighted to make your acquaintance, Miss Wright."

"Thank you, Lord Wessex," she murmured, her eyes fixated on him.

Closing the distance between them, Adam placed his hand on the small of Amelia's back. "You may release Miss Wright's hand now."

Lord Wessex winked before complying. "I apologize for my possessive friend, Miss Wright. He has never done well at allowing others to play with his toys."

With his hand on her back, Adam felt Amelia stiffen at his friend's comment. "Are you implying that I am his plaything?"

The smile slipped from Wessex's face as he realized his error. "My apologies for my insensitive comment. I was merely taking the opportunity to tease my friend."

"Of course," Amelia murmured, turning her attention back to Adam. "Shall we go back inside?"

Lord Wessex held out his hand. "If you will just give me a moment of your time, Miss Wright. I had previously asked Lord Harrington to arrange a meeting so I could ask you a few questions."

"I'm afraid I don't understand," Amelia frowned, casting confused glances between the two men.

"Why did you come to England?" Lord Wessex asked bluntly.

"For an adventure," she answered with an unassuming smile.

Lord Wessex watched her carefully. "And when did you arrive?"

"On the last full moon," she revealed.

"How did you arrive on English soil, Miss Wright?" John asked, crossing his arms over his chest.

Her body tensed, and her expression grew guarded. "Why should it matter to you how I arrived, Lord Wessex?"

"Because no British warship is authorized to carry civilian passengers, and no American merchant ships can pass in British waters without being boarded. So," he paused, "I will ask you again. How did you arrive in England?" Lord Wessex ordered, his tone brooking no argument.

"I don't believe that is what you truly want to ask. Go ahead; ask me what you really want to know," she insisted, tilting her chin up defiantly, her eyes flashing.

With a glimmer of respect, Wessex demanded, "Are you spying for the Americans?"

She laughed lightly as if his words were meant as a joke. "You think I'm a spy?"

Lord Wessex nodded with a serious expression.

All humor left her face as she declared, "No, my lord. I am not a spy."

"Then why, pray tell, are you really here?"

Amelia squared her shoulders. "I am only here to help a friend."

Stepping closer to her, Wessex inquired, "And whom would that friend be?"

"I came to England to help Adam."

Her interrogator's brow lifted in disbelief, his eyes darting between them. "Adam, is it?"

Crossing her arms over her chest defiantly, Amelia retorted, "I have a few questions for *you*, Lord Wessex. Why would I spy for the Americans? Based upon my limited contact with the English people, what would I hope to gain by their friendship?"

Wessex's eyes narrowed dangerously as he took another step to hover over her. "Most likely, you are assigned to befriend lonely lords, using your womanly wiles, in hopes of gaining favors from them. Eventually you will find an official with high enough rank to seduce to achieve your nefarious purpose."

Livid, Amelia dropped her ladylike demeanor. "'Lonely lords'? 'Womanly wiles?'" she sputtered. "How's *this* for a 'nefarious purpose', you *swine!*" Amelia's fist landed squarely in Wessex's face, toppling him to the ground.

"How *dare* you!" she exclaimed, standing over him, trembling with fury.

Amelia then turned her venomous gaze towards Adam. "How dare *both* of you!" She took a step back, putting distance between them. At first, Adam saw the outrage and then the hurt crossing her face as her eyes filled with tears. "I grew up reading stories about English gentlemen, and I always dreamed that I would one day meet one. And now, I find myself with two supposed *gentlemen*, and I realize there is no such thing. It was all a *lie!*"

"Amelia, wait!" Adam pleaded, taking a step closer to her.

Amelia's arm shot out, and her words were shaky. "Don't come any closer, *Lord Harrington*."

"Please, Amelia, it's Adam," he urged in a hushed voice.

Her bottom lip trembled. "No, my lord. You have taught me tonight, once and for all, that we are not friends. Please say goodbye to Marian for me."

Turning on her heel, Amelia marched back towards the ballroom, her back straight, her head held high. Harrington stood still, momentarily frozen in shock, while she disappeared through the glass doors. He had just taken his first step to follow her when a stone-faced Aunt Nellie stepped out onto the veranda.

"Gentlemen. Did you have your fun out here?" she asked icily.

Lord Wessex rose but kept his hand over his reddened left eye. "I was required to ask Miss Wright a few questions."

"Oh, were you?" Aunt Nellie probed, her hands clasped in front of her like a barrier to all her good will. "Did you think of asking me? After all, by accusing Miss Wright of being a spy, you must also believe that I could be capable of harboring a spy."

Before either of them could respond, a very serious Duke of Albany joined them on the veranda and stood beside Aunt Nellie. "Lord Wessex," he boomed, his words slow and deliberate. "Would you care to explain why my wife's dear friend returned to the ballroom in such a delicate state?"

Adam watched as his friend's resolve shrank, but Wessex managed to answer the duke's question directly. "I was simply inquiring about her association with the Americans during this time of war, Your Grace."

The duke's jaw clenched tightly. "I hope that you did not just imply that my wife and I would ever associate with an American spy?"

"Most emphatically not, Your Grace!" Wessex replied hastily.

"That is an appropriate answer, Wessex, because I will vouch for Miss Wright," the duke proclaimed, leaving no room for discussion.

Bowing, Wessex confirmed, "The matter will be dropped at once, Your Grace."

"See that it is," the duke growled. "And I'd better not hear of anyone harassing Miss Wright again, is that clear?" His words were firm, and the warning in his tone spoke volumes.

Turning his disapproving glare towards Adam, he grunted. "How could you stand by and not defend her honor?"

"I, too, stand most humbly corrected, Your Grace," Adam admitted, also bowing.

"I have eyes, Harrington," the duke said, his words softening just a touch. "It is clear that you hold Miss Wright in high regard, but you disappointed her tonight." With a shake of his head, the duke turned back towards the ballroom and disappeared through the open door.

Aunt Nellie, too, shook her head regretfully. "Goodnight, gentlemen." She hesitated. "And I use that term lightly."

Adam watched miserably as Aunt Nellie returned to the ballroom, and he dropped his head in shame. What had just transpired? One moment he was about to declare his intentions to Amelia, and the next he was being dismissed from the ball by the Duke of Albany and Aunt Nellie.

"I say, that went rather poorly, Harrington. I do apologize for ruining the evening," John mumbled as his hand gently probed his eye. "However, we now know that Miss Wright isn't a spy."

Unable to resist, Adam punched his friend in the other eye.

Laura Beers

Chapter 11

Standing at the bay window in his study, Adam stared out towards the east lawn. During the past four days, his mood had soured at the mere thought of what had transpired on that veranda. Remembering the look of betrayal on Amelia's face, he slammed the palm of his hand against the window sill.

Despite sending hundreds of flowers along with apology notes to Twickenham Manor, Amelia still refused to see him when he came to call. It had been four days. Four long days without even a glimpse of her. Why had he taken her smile or laugh for granted?

Turning back to his desk, he moved to his chair and slumped down. Would Amelia ever forgive him? For that matter, would he ever see her again?

Mr. Blake walked into the room with a stack of papers in his hand. "Your quarterly reports, milord." He approached the desk and extended the papers towards his master. "Your horse has been readied, per your request."

"Thank you, Blake." Lord Harrington accepted the papers and dropped them onto the pile of correspondence. "I suppose I should be off then," he stated, knowing it was a foolhardy thing to attempt to call on Amelia for the second time today.

With a concerned glance, Mr. Blake asked, "Are you feeling well, milord?"

"That will be all, Blake," the earl responded in his usual gruff voice.

Mr. Blake nodded thoughtfully as he started towards the open door. Suddenly, he stopped and retraced his steps. "If I may say," he began slowly, "I cannot help but comment on how the staff misses Miss Wright."

Leaning forward in his seat, Adam put his elbows on his desk and clasped his hands together, his fingers forming a steeple. "There is nothing I can do on that matter, and frankly, it is neither their business, nor yours."

"Very well, milord," Mr. Blake said, straightening to his full height. "It's just that... Miss Wright brought joy and laughter back to this estate, and we are loathe to see..."

"To see what, Blake?" Harrington asked dryly.

"To see the dark depression return, milord," Mr. Blake expressed. "I have worked for this estate since you were a child, and we all experienced hardships when Lady Harrington died."

He frowned. "Yes, and...?"

Mr. Blake took a deep breath and forged ahead. "Forgive me, milord, but you have managed to let it define you."

"How dare you presume..."

Mr. Blake cut him off, shocking him into silence. "This may cost me my position, but I will say what I have come to say, and I insist that you listen! I have always hoped that the love of your daughter would break your unhappy cycle. It pains me to admit that I was wrong. You shut her away in the nursery and had the nursemaids raise her." He took a step and leaned towards Adam paternally. "Then Miss Wright arrived, and Miss Marian befriended her. Can you not imagine, milord, what joy it is at last to hear a child's sweet laughter echoing throughout these lonely halls?"

White-lipped but silent, Adam waited for Blake to finish his thought like a prisoner awaiting the fall of a guillotine.

His faithful and normally stoic servant continued, "Now, I see glimpses of the father that you were meant to be; the father that Lady Harrington would have wanted you to be. And Miss Wright did that. She has matched you wit for wit and made you a better person."

Dropping his arms, Adam sighed, deflated. "I know all of this, Blake. But Miss Wright is refusing to see me."

Mr. Blake huffed impatiently. "You would give her up that easily then?"

"I am not giving up!" Adam shouted, jumping to his feet so forcefully that he overturned his chair.

Mr. Blake came towards the desk and held his master's irate gaze with dignity. "Miss Wright may refuse to see you, but she rides out every day around this time to check on Mrs. Stevens."

"She does? How do you know this, Blake?"

The butler gave a short nod and pronounced, "It is my duty to be aware of all the comings and goings on this estate, milord. I have never before met a lady quite like Miss Wright. She is bold, fearless, and has a tender heart for the less fortunate. In addition, she is blessed with a keen eye, a quick wit..."

"And a strong right hook." Adam grinned. "I couldn't agree with you more."

"Now that's more like it! That's the stuff! I strongly urge you to go to her, milord; go and claim your lovely lady," Mr. Blake encouraged. "The cook has prepared a basket for you to deliver to Mrs. Stevens." He gave Adam an exaggerated wink. "After all, Miss Wright won't refuse your company if she believes you are going to call on the Stevens family."

With new resolve, Lord Harrington quickly buttoned his coat and straightened his cravat. "Before I go, Blake, answer me this: are my servants conspiring for me to wed Miss Wright?"

Mr. Blake cleared his throat before replying, "To be frank, milord, I believe the whole staff may quit if Miss Wright does not become the mistress of Belmont Manor."

Adam furrowed his brow. "I do hope you're not serious."

In response, Mr. Blake raised an eyebrow, gave him a knowing smile, and walked out of the study.

Shortly, Lord Harrington was galloping his chestnut gelding down the road towards Bexmore. As he came around the bend, he saw a single female rider trotting along the side of the road. Even though the woman was wearing a bonnet, he immediately recognized Amelia.

Slowing his horse's gait, he approached her and started riding side-by-side. "Good afternoon, Miss Wright," he declared in a cheerful voice.

"What are you doing here, Lord Harrington?" she inquired, not looking at him.

"I am off to visit the Stevenses."

She turned her head towards him, eyeing him in suspicion. "You are? Why?"

He held up the basket in his left hand. "To deliver a basket of food my cook prepared."

"That is kind of you," she murmured.

He smiled at her, ignoring her look of blatant annoyance. "And where are you riding this fine morning?" he questioned innocently.

"To the Stevens's, as well," she replied, reluctantly.

The persistent earl hooked the basket to the pommel of his saddle. "Then I propose we ride together since we have the same destination."

"I would rather not, my lord," she stated through clenched teeth.

Pretending he didn't hear her, Harrington pressed forward. "This will give me adequate time to apologize for what happened at the duke's ball."

Amelia kicked her horse to increase its speed, but his horse easily matched hers. "Go away, Lord Harrington!" she demanded, barely sparing him a glance.

"I could," he started, "but I would rather stay and enjoy your company."

Amelia pulled her horse to a stop and turned to face him. "I have no wish to speak to you ever again. You sat back and allowed Lord Wessex to disrespect me most horrendously."

Reining back his horse, he recited his rehearsed explanation, "Wessex started an investigation when he discovered that two beautiful American women had suddenly showed up in England, with no explanation. We are, after all, in a skirmish with America."

"'Beautiful American women'?"

"Anyone with eyes can see how truly exquisite you are." He gave her a roguish smile. "And I, for one, could understand why he thought you were a spy."

Amelia tensed. "And why is that?"

"Because you have managed to bewitch me from our very first encounter," he confessed.

"And now?" she asked hesitantly. "Do you still think I am capable of being a spy?"

"No," he shared, gazing into her gold-flecked eyes, "and Wessex does not either."

"Aunt Nellie told me that the duke caused Lord Wessex to shake in his boots." She giggled and brought her gloved hand up to cover her mouth.

"He did," Adam replied, savoring the sound of her laughter, "and he made it clear that under no circumstances were you and Miss Turner to be bothered again."

"How does the duke wield so much power?"

Adam ran his hand down his horse's neck. "The Duke of Albany has both vast wealth and great favor with the Prince Regent. His word is law around here."

Kicking her horse back into a trot, Amelia started back down the road. "I will have to thank him when I meet with the duchess."

"You are meeting with the Duchess of Albany?" he asked in disbelief.

"She invited Miss Turner and me over for tea," she shared casually.

Impressed, Adam whistled as he reached into his basket and pulled out a biscuit. "That is a high honor," he expressed before he took a bite of the delicious treat.

"What are you doing?" Amelia admonished. "That food is for the Stevenses."

Plopping the rest of the biscuit into his mouth, he reached into the basket and pulled out another one. He extended it towards her as he explained, "My cook supplied extra biscuits in hopes that it would entice you to speak to me."

Reaching her hand out with a wry smile, she accepted the biscuit and quickly took a bite. Her eyes widened with pleasure.

"This cookie is fantastic!"

"Cookie?"

"My apologies, I meant biscuit," she corrected as she finished the treat.

"Does accepting the biscuit mean you accept my apology for being a ninnyhammer, Miss Wright?" he asked hopefully.

Wiping crumbs from her gloves, she remarked primly, "Well... I never actually *heard* an apology, Lord Harrington."

Bringing his horse closer, he reached for her reins and stopped their horses in the road. "Miss Wright," he hesitated, as his eyes implored hers, "please accept my most humble apology for not protecting you when you needed it most."

He watched as her eyes softened, making them so irresistibly beautiful.

An impish smile widened her lips before she said, "I suppose I must, because Twickenham Manor cannot possibly handle any more influxes of flowers."

Adam chuckled. "Does this also mean you will call me Adam again?"

"I will," she paused, lifting her brow, "under one condition."

"Whatever you desire," he breathed, knowing he would do anything to hear his name on her lips again.

Amelia's eyes shifted towards the basket. "Will you please give me another of those amazing biscuits... Adam?"

He laughed. "Agreed."

Reaching into the basket, he pulled out another biscuit and handed it to her. Only this time, his gloved hand gently traced her fingers, and he was pleased to hear the sharp intake of her breath. Releasing the biscuit, he leaned back and encouraged his horse to resume its walk.

The courtship of Miss Amelia Wright had just begun.

As they walked along the road towards Bexmore, it appeared that neither Amelia nor Adam was in a hurry to arrive at their destination.

Listening to Adam's adventures while at Eton, Amelia found herself laughing at his boyhood antics. After he shared how he brought a frog into his class, she asked, "And let me guess, your headmaster caned you?"

Adam nodded. "My classmates and I were caned on a regular basis."

"How awful it must have been for you to be away from your parents at such a young age," she murmured.

"Not particularly," he replied. "Most sons of the peerage are sent away to boarding school when they turn thirteen." He adjusted the reins in his hands. "Tell me about America."

Amelia sighed. He was asking about how America was in 1813 and not two hundred years in the future. She decided to tell him the partial truth. "It is the land of opportunity," she started. "Women are treated as equals with men, and we are free to pursue our educational interests."

"And men allow their wives to work?" Adam asked.

Amelia let out a soft chuckle. "Women are free to see to their own lives as necessary. Some women even choose not to marry and maintain full control over their lives."

"Why would a woman want to remain a spinster?"

"We don't use that term where I am from," she shared. "And for some women, their careers are more important than family."

Adam frowned. "You don't think that way, do you?"

"No," she admitted softly. "My parents were not only devoted and kind, but they were deeply in love with each other." She gave him a weak smile. "It always warmed my heart to see the way they looked at each other. It was always filled with such longing."

"And do you wish to marry?"

"I do, but only when I find the right person," she revealed. "I want a man that will love me more than anything else."

Watching her with an intensity that she did not understand, Adam replied softly, "Any man would be a fool not to treasure you above all else."

She chuckled. "You say that, but I have been on some pretty bad dates."

"Dates?" he asked.

"Um… courting," she corrected in a rush.

"If men have attempted to court you, then why are you still unwed at the age of seven and twenty?" Adam inquired with frank but respectful curiosity.

"That is not too old where I am from," she defended in a huff. "Besides, I suppose I have been too busy studying to become a doctor to have time to focus on my personal life."

Adam shifted his gaze towards the road. "I still find it an odd choice for a woman to even want to become a doctor."

"And I find it odd that gentlemen don't assist in raising their children here," she challenged with an uplifted brow.

With a decisive nod, he brought his gaze back towards her. "I agree. I am going to start taking a more active role in Marian's life."

"Really? That pleases me."

"Yes," he said, his eyes holding her captive. "I would also like permission to start courting you."

Amelia just gaped at him for a moment before pulling back on the reins, hoping he was not in earnest. "You can't possibly be serious, Adam."

"I am." He followed her lead and stopped his horse. "I have grown to care for you, and I hope to win your favor."

She shook her head. "You couldn't possibly have grown to care for me to such a degree so quickly. Isn't that like a marriage contract in England?"

"If you agree to the courtship, then it is akin to an engagement," he revealed.

"My answer is absolutely no," she stated.

He smiled at her. "We shall see."

"You must understand that I am leaving on the night of the next full moon," she reminded him. "I have no intention of staying in England."

"What if I gave you a reason to stay?" he asked intently.

Shifting her gaze over his shoulder at the countryside, she replied, "My life is back in America. Regardless of my feelings for you, I need to go home."

"You have feelings for me?" he probed with a devilish gleam in his eyes.

Drat! "I care for you as well," she admitted, "but that does not translate to courting. It takes years for people to fall in love."

"I disagree."

"What specifically do you disagree about?"

"I believe a person can fall in love in a moment, and it can last for a lifetime."

"Was it love at first sight with Agnes?" she asked.

"It was," he responded, his eyes growing reflective. "Recently, I have come to believe a heart can learn to love more than one person."

Up ahead was the Stevens's cottage, and she could see Mr. Stevens outside chopping wood. Kicking her horse into a run, Amelia decided she was finished with this ridiculous conversation. What was Adam thinking by asking permission to court her? He was ruining everything. They were only friends.

Despite him being ruggedly handsome, clever, witty, and the most interesting man she had ever met, she refused to encourage him. She was going home to her time. There was no way that she would ever choose to remain living in an era that didn't have indoor plumbing.

Sinking the ax into the chopping block with a mighty heave, Henry raised his hand in greeting as they approached. At some point, Adam caught up with her.

Once they reined in their horses, Adam dismounted effortlessly and came around his horse towards her. He put his hands on her waist and smiled as she stiffened. "Please allow me to assist you in dismounting your horse."

"But I don't need assistance, Adam," she murmured, attempting to ignore the tingles cascading through her body at his touch.

"Amelia," he persisted gently, not relinquishing his hold on her waist, "do allow me the honor of assisting you."

The way her name rolled off his lips made her feel precious. "As you wish, my lord."

Placing her hands on his shoulders, he ever so gently assisted her off her horse and didn't release his hold until she was firmly on the ground.

"Thank you, Amelia. It brings me great joy to be so close to you," he murmured softly.

Unable to speak through the sudden rush of emotion coursing through her, Amelia took a deep breath and brushed past, carefully negotiating the woodchips on her way.

She regained her composure as she approached the blacksmith and inquired, "How is your wife faring today, Mr. Stevens?"

"Please, come inside, Miss Wright, Milord 'Arrington," Mr. Stevens said eagerly, ushering them inside his cottage.

The proud father stepped aside, grinning widely. Amelia observed that Amy was sitting up on the round stool with her back leaning against the wall. The sleeping baby lay swaddled in a simple wooden cradle beside her. The new mother was knitting a stocking, but she lowered it to her lap and smiled when she saw them. "You are spoilin' us with your daily visits, Miss Wright, an' that's the truth of it."

Standing up gingerly, Amy placed her knitting back onto the stool as Adam ducked through the door. Her eyes grew wide as her gaze shifted over Amelia's shoulder. "Lord 'Arrington, milord," she said respectfully as she curtsied awkwardly. "Welcome to our modest 'ome."

Adam nodded his acknowledgement, extending the basket towards Amy. "My cook sent a basket over with some victuals."

"A thousand thanks to ye an' your cook, milord," Amy replied, placing the basket onto the table. "Er… this is the second basket sent from your estate today."

"It is?" the earl's voice rose nearly an octave, and his eyebrows shot to the top of his forehead.

Henry gave his wife a nervous glance. "Mr. Blake's orders, milord. A footman has delivered a basket 'ere every day since my wife's... uh... surgery."

To Amelia's surprise, Adam smiled. "That is wonderful news. I must thank Mr. Blake for his due diligence."

Amy breathed a sigh of relief. "Them baskets been nothin' short of a godsend, milord, since I've been unable to do me usual chores."

Admiring the sleeping infant, Amelia asked, "May I hold her?"

"Oh, yes, miss, you'd honor us that much, ye would," the blacksmith's wife allowed.

Picking up the sleeping infant, Amelia took a moment to smell the delightful aroma of the newborn. As she cradled the baby in her arms, swaying back and forth on her feet in the way women have done since time began, she felt a twinge of longing for a family. She had always wanted children, but it had always been her secondary focus. For so long, all she had ever wanted to be was a doctor. Would she ever find the time for a family?

Lifting her gaze, she saw that Adam was watching her, his eyes full of tenderness. Their gazes locked, sharing an intimate moment. Her breath caught in her throat, and she had a hard time swallowing. It was as if he knew what she was thinking.

Turning towards Amy, she asked, "May I examine you in the other room?"

"I suppose so," Amy agreed.

Amelia handed the infant to Henry and smiled. "This will only take a moment."

After entering the tiny bedroom, Amelia closed the door behind her and took the time to examine the scar on Amy's abdomen. Once finished, she shared the good news. "I don't see any sign of infection, and this wound is healing very nicely. In a few days, I will remove the stitches, and you will be free to resume your regular activities, but please use some caution at first. Don't lift anything heavier than the baby for two more weeks."

"We can't thank you enough, Miss Wright…" Amy started sniffing and blinking rapidly.

"You don't have to thank me," Amelia assured her with a shake of her head. "I did what needed to be done, that is all."

Amy's eyes twinkled with merriment. "How nice that Lord 'Arrington 'imself escorted you to our cottage, aint it, miss?"

"He happened to catch up with me on the ride over, and we decided to ride together," she explained, hoping to downplay the significance.

"Of course, miss," Amy replied with a cheeky wink.

Opening the door between the two rooms, Amelia saw that Lord Harrington and Mr. Stevens were outside. In a strange reversal of roles, it appeared that Adam was chopping wood as Henry looked on, cradling his infant in his arms and cooing as fathers do.

Walking outside, Amelia stopped short at the unexpected sight of Adam's muscular physique as he brought the ax down, causing a loud, splintering crash of wood. At some point, he had taken off both his riding coat and his waistcoat and draped them on a crude wood fence at the edge of the blacksmith's garden.

Mr. Stevens saw his wife and smiled tenderly. "'Ave ye told 'er the good news yet?"

Amy shook her head. "I was 'oping to tell 'er together, 'Enry."

"What good news?" Amelia asked, reluctantly prying her eyes off Adam.

Proudly, Amy announced, "We've decided to name our little wee babe Amelia, after you, Miss Wright."

Touched by their kindness, she replied, "Thank you. I am honored."

Draping his free arm over his wife's shoulder, Mr. Stevens expressed, "If it warn't for ye, miss, me wife and babe would've died that awful night. I can't even begin to thank ye…" His voice faltered. "Your name'll always be spoken with rev'rence in our 'ome."

Her eyes brimmed with tears at their heartfelt words, and she blinked back her emotions. "You are both too kind. I thank you for your trust as well."

Feeling a hand on the small of her back, Amelia felt comforted by Adam's touch. "Are you ready for me to escort you back to Twickenham Manor?" he asked.

She shook her head. "No, let's stop by Belmont Manor and play a game with Marian."

"Now that sounds like a grand idea," he said, smiling down at her, causing her heart to suddenly flop over.

This time, as their eyes met, Amelia realized with a shock that she was in deep trouble. At some point, and completely unintentionally, she had fallen in love with Lord Harrington!

Laura Beers

Chapter 12

Two days later, Amelia was sitting contentedly in the library of Twickenham Manor with a stack of books piled high on the table next to her. She felt like a little girl in a candy store as she debated which book to read first. It was a tough choice, considering these prints were all in a museum in her day.

Running her fingers over the spines, she murmured, "What to read? What to read?"

"*Gulliver's Travels, Candide, Robinson Crusoe, A Modest Proposal, Moll Flanders,*" she started listing.

A voice broke through her musings. "Miss Wright, your presence is requested in the drawing room," a young fae informed her.

Lifting her head, she asked, "By whom?"

"You'll see," was her vague reply as she turned to leave the room.

Rising from the camelback settee, Amelia took a moment to smooth out her Pomona green dress, the color reminding her of a tart, green apple. Despite the many layers of clothing she wore under the gown, she had to admit this might be her favorite part of this adventure. The dresses made her feel so feminine.

Walking down the hall, she stopped at a mirror and admired her reflection. Marie had done an amazing job of pinning her hair to the side in an elaborate hairstyle, and strands of hair were curled around her face. Despite not wearing makeup, she felt beautiful.

Her parents, friends, and colleagues had always told her that she was attractive, but she had never believed them. But the way Adam looked at her made her feel like a queen. She pondered that thought as she headed towards the drawing room.

Striding into the drawing room, her steps faltered when she saw a finely dressed Lord Wessex standing near the mantle, and he appeared to be in a staring contest with Peyton, only her eyes were narrowed to slits.

Taking a moment to observe Lord Wessex, she had to admit that he did bear an uncanny resemblance to her mother's nurse, Dustin. They must be distant relatives, she mused.

Ignoring proper Regency etiquette, she drawled sarcastically, "Oh, good. Lord Wessex has come for a visit."

Adam's amused voice came from behind her. "I hope I fare a better reception than Lord Wessex."

Spinning around, she saw Lord Harrington leaning against the wall, dressed in a blue riding coat, primrose waistcoat, and buff trousers. "Why were you hiding there?" she asked him.

He chuckled, as he pushed off the wall. "My job was to ensure you didn't run away once you saw Lord Wessex."

"I must admit I was tempted," she admitted. "Although, I don't understand why Miss Turner is staring daggers at him."

Adam walked up next to her and leaned in, allowing her to take in his scent of musk and leather, which was quickly becoming her favorite smell.

"You missed Lord Wessex informing Miss Turner that the home office has officially stopped the inquiry of her being a spy."

"How gracious of him," she replied, finding herself drawing closer to Adam.

He gave her the crooked grin that she had become quite fond of. "And Miss Turner's response was similar to the one you had at the ball."

Peyton huffed, "When Amelia informed me that you accused her of being a spy, I didn't believe a man could be so thickheaded."

Instead of appearing offended, Lord Wessex stepped over to Miss Turner's chair and placed his arms on the armrests, leaning in to her. "It's not every day that I am insulted by such a lovely lady."

To Amelia's surprise, she saw Peyton blush, but she maintained eye contact with Lord Wessex. "Well, it's not every day that I am accused of being a spy," she replied, cheekily.

"Did you miss the part where I called you lovely?" Lord Wessex added in a rather hoarse voice.

Watching this peculiar interaction, Amelia found she was enjoying Adam's nearness, oblivious to the fact that Aunt Nellie had just walked into the room. "Lord Wessex, please remember that you are a guest in my home. You will treat my other guests in a dignified fashion," she declared harshly.

Lord Wessex pushed off the armrest and turned to face the matron of the manor. "I apologize, Aunt Nellie. I was just taking a moment to apologize to Miss Turner."

"Interesting," Aunt Nellie murmured. "It appeared that you were accosting the dear girl."

"That was not my intention," Lord Wessex insisted, boldly winking at Miss Turner.

Aunt Nellie lowered herself onto a floral, upholstered armchair. "When I was informed that you and Lord Harrington came to call, I thought it had been a mistake," she stated. "Pray tell, what are your intentions for this visit, gentlemen?"

Wiping a smile off her face, Amelia glanced at Adam, waiting to see his reaction. He was watching her, and his lips were twitching. For a moment, she enjoyed their private interlude but heard Aunt Nellie clear her throat, drawing their attention back to the group.

Taking a step forward, Lord Harrington put more distance between them as he explained, "Lord Wessex and I hope that Miss Turner and Miss Wright are amendable to spending the rest of the day with us."

Aunt Nellie lifted her brow. "And why would they agree to that?"

Lord Wessex gave her an apologetic smile. "I am hoping to make up for my inappropriate actions. I was overzealous in my approach to discover the truth. It was not fair of me to assume that Miss Turner and Miss Wright were spies solely because they are American."

"And based upon the fact that Miss Wright performed a caesarian delivery," Adam interjected, giving her a private smile.

Aunt Nellie leaned back in her seat, her eyes assessing them. "What do you have scheduled?"

"It is a surprise," Lord Wessex shared.

"Ladies," Aunt Nellie said. "What do you think? Are you agreeable?"

Peyton nodded. "I think it would be fun," she admitted, warranting a smile from Lord Wessex.

"As do I," Amelia confirmed.

"Very well," Aunt Nellie replied, standing up. "I hope you have an enjoyable time." Stepping over to Lord Harrington, she patted him on the shoulder. "It is good to see you so happy, Adam."

The group watched Aunt Nellie depart, and Amelia turned her expectant gaze to Lord Harrington. "What do you have planned?"

Adam came to stand in front of her, reaching for her ungloved hand and bringing it up to his lips. As he held her gaze, his lips kissed her knuckles. His lips were warm and lingered on her skin, causing shivers to cascade down her body. He grinned up at her. "Adventure."

"Adventure?" she breathed, unsure of his meaning.

His smile turned roguish. "You came to England for an adventure, remember?"

Good heavens! She couldn't seem to think clearly with him standing so close.

"I did," she stammered.

Turning back to include Lord Wessex, Adam revealed, "We are going to take you on a tour of London."

Sitting on the edge of her seat, Amelia sat across from Adam in the swaying carriage, her face tilting away from him, staring out the window, but he could still see the wonder in her eyes. The stuffy coach and the smell of the River Thames seemed to do little to diminish her excitement.

The carriage jerked to a stop near the waterfront, and Adam watched as Amelia turned towards him.

"Are we going on a boat?"

Adam placed his hand out of the window and opened the carriage door, not bothering to wait for the footman. "I hope you are not afraid of water," he said as he hopped out of the carriage.

Amelia extended her hand towards him. "I'm not."

"Excellent. We are going to take a wherry." Adam took her arm and placed it in the crook of his, leading her towards a group of red and green boats.

Looking puzzled, Amelia asked, "I've heard of a ferry, but what's a wherry?"

Adam grinned. "It's a sharp-bowed skiff used to carry passengers."

"Oars, oars!" the watermen started shouting.

Adam pointed towards a red wherry, ignoring the uncouth jests coming from the watermen. "We are going to Vauxhall Gardens." He jumped onto the skiff. "Have you been there before?"

"No," she admitted, as he held out his hand to help her onto the bobbing boat, "but I have read books that mention them."

Adam held out his hand to assist Miss Turner into the skiff. Once she was seated next to Amelia, Lord Wessex stepped down, and the waterman manning their wherry started rowing towards the gardens.

"Why does London smell so awful?" Miss Turner asked, placing her gloved hand up to her nose.

Before he could explain, Amelia replied, "What you are smelling is a combination of the trash accumulating on the streets, poor sanitary conditions, and the human excrement that is dumped into the River Thames."

The men stared at Amelia for a moment, then Adam broke the silence. "Have you been to the rookeries before?"

"No." She flashed him a bright smile. "I read a book about it."

Adam placed his hand on the edge of the boat. "You described it perfectly."

"I have always been fascinated by London," she revealed. "My mother is English, and we used to spend our summers here."

The skiff tilted to the left as Lord Wessex reached out to hold the side of the boat. "I was not aware that you had a familial connection in England."

"You didn't ask," Amelia teased.

Lord Wessex laughed. "*Touché*, Miss Wright."

Amelia's smile faded, and a sadness passed over her, briefly dimming her whole countenance. Her eyes drifted over the river, and Adam leaned forward, placing his hand over her clasped hands. Rather than jerking her hands back, her gaze returned to him. She offered him a grateful smile.

"Sorry, I'm afraid I was woolgathering."

Peyton smiled over at her. "Woolgathering, huh?"

"When in London, do as the Londoners do," Amelia said, returning her friend's smile.

Adam looked over at Lord Wessex, who just shrugged at him. "How long have you two been friends?" he asked.

Amelia gave Peyton a sidelong glance before answering, "About two weeks?"

"You seem close," Lord Wessex commented.

"We arrived at Twickenham Manor on the same night," Peyton explained.

The waterman ferried them to the wall near Vauxhall Gardens. Lord Wessex stepped out and assisted the women out of the wherry, his hand lingering on Miss Turner's.

The sun was starting to dip past the horizon as Adam paid the waterman. He offered his arm to Amelia as he said, "I hope you don't mind, but we planned to eat supper here."

"I do not mind at all," Amelia replied, tucking her arm into the crook of his, leaning into him.

After paying their admission, they strolled inside and heard the orchestras warming up. The walkways and fountains were illuminated with brightly lit lamps, leading them to both temples and saloons.

As much as he was enjoying the sights of the gardens, it paled in comparison to the light in Amelia's golden-flecked eyes as she saw things for the first time. He chuckled as she refused to stroll at a ladylike pace. She seemed to absorb everything that she read or saw and wanted more.

Leading Amelia back towards where the suppers were served, he asked, "Are you enjoying yourself?"

"I could spend weeks here without getting bored," she said in an excited tone.

He chuckled. "Where would you sleep?"

Lifting her head up to the sky, she replied, "Under the canopy of heaven."

Directing her towards an empty alcove, Adam waited till she took a seat at the table before sitting next to her. "If you stayed in England, then you could visit Vauxhall Gardens every day."

"I wish," she murmured, "but… I have responsibilities at home."

"Which are?" he pressed.

Amelia's eyes strayed towards a lovely soprano singing with the orchestra. "The two most pressing are my mother's ailing health and my career."

A servant girl placed a plate of a cold supper in front of them and two glasses of punch, as he carefully phrased his next words. "What if you didn't have to work to support yourself?"

"I assume I would volunteer my time as a doctor to help others," she responded, reaching for a piece of thin ham.

"But what if you didn't have to work as a doctor?"

Amelia turned to face him, the light of the lamps illuminating her face. "You seem to think that I choose to work as a doctor just because I need an income."

He cocked his head quizzically. "Is that not true? Why else would you do so, if not to earn a living?"

With a slight shake of her head, she revealed, "I have come from a long line of doctors, both male and female, and I chose to be a doctor because I am passionate about helping people."

Adam saw several emotions flitter across her face before she asked, "Why do you help your tenants, Adam?" She lifted her brow knowingly. "Do you help them because it is a duty, or do you help them because you care about them?"

Adam shrugged. "I suppose it is a little of both."

"I've worked hard for many years to become a doctor," Amelia confessed. "It is who I am."

"And I respect that, but you can't work as a doctor in England," he informed her, reaching for a piece of ham.

"I know," she replied after taking a sip of her punch, "which is why I must return home."

"You should stay," he said in a surprisingly steady voice.

Amelia shook her head. "I can't. I don't belong here."

"Stay with me," he requested. It sounded bold enough to almost be a command.

She tilted her head to one side and studied him, a small crease appearing between her brows. "What exactly are you asking me?"

As he opened his mouth, John and Miss Turner walked into the alcove. "There you are," John proclaimed. "We thought we had lost you."

After they were situated, Miss Turner accepted a piece of thin ham from the plate that Harrington offered, and her eyes grew wide with pleasure. "This ham is amazing."

With a side-glance at Amelia, he saw that her body was tense, and she remained fixated on the entertainment, clearly refusing to look at him. *Bollocks!* He had spoken too soon.

He studied her, admiring the rosiness of her cheeks. It was apparent that Amelia was not immune to his charms, but he would need to convince her that he was worth the risk.

Why were women such perplexing creatures? What if Amelia didn't have feelings for him, and he was on a fool's errand?

Well then, a fool he would be.

0

Chapter 13

Walking down the path from Twickenham Manor to the River Thames, Adam's words, "Stay with me," echoed in Amelia's mind. She wondered what he was thinking. I can't stay with him, she thought. This is not my time.

Stopping at the shoreline, Amelia stared out over the water. She was on the cusp of obtaining everything that she had worked so hard to achieve. She couldn't throw that all away to stay in an unfamiliar time with a man that she had just met. No, that was unfathomable.

She sighed as she tucked a few loose hairs behind her ears. Then why was she even considering it? She had never experienced emotions this intense with any man, and it frightened her. Perhaps she could stay for another full moon. No, that was not a good idea. Either way, she would be delaying the inevitable. She had to go back to her time.

"Amelia," a familiar voice said behind her; a voice that managed to penetrate all her waking thoughts.

Keeping her stiff back to him, Amelia was not surprised when she heard the dry leaves crunch under his boots as he approached. Her mind told her to flee, but her heart told her to stay.

"Where have you been these past three days?" Adam asked as he came to stand next to her, keeping his gaze straight ahead. He was dressed in riding attire, but he wore no top hat.

"I have been… occupied," she replied vaguely, not feeling strong enough to look over at him. Whenever she looked into his piercing blue eyes, her resolve would shrink, and she needed to keep her wits about her.

"I see." He made a clucking noise with his tongue. "Silly me. I had wrongly assumed that you were avoiding me because I asked you to stay in England with me."

Amelia pressed her lips tightly together, not knowing how to respond. How could she possibly express what she felt when she doubted her own emotions?

Without saying a word, Adam's right hand encompassed hers tenderly. She turned, keeping her gaze trained on their hands.

"I can't stay," she murmured. "I have to go home."

His other hand trailed down her arm until he encompassed her other hand. "I care for you, Amelia."

"And I care for you as well," she replied, finally bringing her eyes up to his.

"Stay. Allow me to court you properly." His eyes implored hers.

Tears came to her eyes, but she blinked them away. "I have to go home to take care of my mother," she replied softly, "and I don't want to give up being a doctor."

"We will go together and bring your mother back to my estate, where I will hire staff to care for her." Adam stepped closer. "And if you marry me, you won't ever need to worry about funds again."

A tear started rolling down her cheek, and she wished for the first time that things could be different. "You must understand; if I stay, I would be giving up everything."

Releasing her right hand, he gently wiped away her tear. "If you stay, you would never regret it. I will give you whatever your heart desires. You will want for nothing."

"What I am speaking of is not material wealth," she tried to explain. "I would be giving up my independence. My entire identity."

"You would be a countess," he countered.

Amelia lowered her gaze to the lapels of his riding coat. "A title is of little importance to me."

"I supposed as much." Adam's words were filled with pain.

Hearing the anguish in his voice, Amelia brought her hand up to cup his cheek. "You are a good man, and I hope you have a lifetime of happiness. But it won't be with me."

His eyes crinkled as he watched her. "Why am I not enough?"

"It has nothing to do with you," she insisted. "I don't belong in your world."

"I don't accept that." His words became firm. "You may deny your feelings, but I won't let you go without a fight."

"You must," she pleaded.

He gave her a tender smile. "I am going to kiss you now, Miss Amelia Wright."

"I wish you wouldn't," she whispered, knowing she was lying to herself. She wanted him to kiss her.

Lowering his head, he kept his gaze fixed on her, giving her ample time to protest, but she had no willpower to resist him. Then, he kissed her tenderly, carefully, sweetly, still giving her the chance to push him away. Never had she imagined that a kiss could be so all-encompassing, giving her the intense desire to never let him go.

Placing his arms around her waist, Adam pulled her tightly against him, and she surrendered to his touch. As she brought her arms up around his neck, she threaded her fingers through his thick hair.

"Amelia," he whispered against her lips, "you have no idea what you do to me."

Not wanting this moment to end, she lifted on her tiptoes to press her lips to his. She didn't want to waste another moment together. Adam took control and deepened the kiss, making her want to forget all the reasons why she couldn't be with him. She kissed him back with matching fervor, knowing that this moment would be engrained forever in her heart.

Adam broke the kiss, bringing his forehead to rest on hers. "How can you kiss me like that and still want to leave me?" he asked, his voice breathless. "Make me understand."

"I can't." She couldn't tell him about the magic at Twickenham Manor without first asking permission from Aunt Nellie.

Keeping his arms around her, he said, "Come with me to the opera tonight. I have also secured tickets for Miss Turner and Lord Wessex."

"I don't…"

Her words were cut off when his lips pressed against hers, which was a most pleasing way to be interrupted.

"I won't take no for an answer," he asserted in a hoarse voice.

She smiled. "If that is the case…"

He kissed her again, this time his lips lingered longer on hers. "I thought I heard a refusal on your lips," he said with a lopsided grin.

Returning his grin, she replied, "I am not complaining."

"Then I will call on you tonight."

"Yes, please." She laughed softly because his hold on her tightened. "But now you have to let me go."

"Do I?"

Stepping out of his arms, she laughed again at his crestfallen expression. "You do. I am having afternoon tea with the Duchess of Albany."

"When must you depart?" He took a step closer to her, his eyes holding merriment.

"Why?" she asked curiously.

He waggled his brow. "I am wondering how long I can spend with you before I must escort you back to Twickenham Manor."

Accepting his offered arm, Amelia leaned into him. "Perhaps you could show me the long path back home."

Why did those words sound so enticing?

Walking into the Duchess of Albany's drawing room with Peyton and Aunt Nellie, Amelia was greeted by the words, "Welcome to my humble home."

"Humble?" Amelia chuckled, choosing to sit on a red velvet settee across from the duchess.

"Yes, you should see the size of our country estate in Bath," the duchess replied merrily.

Peyton sat down next to her. "Good heavens, how do you manage to live in such horrendous conditions?"

The duchess ran her fingers over the rich upholstery. "This is a far cry from the pig farm where I was raised in Wyoming."

Sitting down gracefully next to the duchess, Aunt Nellie said, "Thank you for the invitation for tea."

The duchess smiled. "Thank you for accepting it." She rose and closed the door. "Now, tell me everything about the future."

Peyton leaned forward in her seat. "We now carry around computers in our hands and call them laptops."

"We have made remarkable medical advances in the past few years," Amelia shared.

The duchess waved her hand. "What I am more concerned about is who did Rachel end up with on *Friends*?"

"The television show *Friends*?" Amelia laughed.

"Yes, I faithfully watched that show for four years, and many times I have wondered about the outcome," the duchess revealed.

Peyton clasped her hands in her lap. "Rachel ended up with Ross, but only after they had a baby together."

"Oh my," the duchess expressed, placing her hand over her chest, "you must tell me everything."

After Peyton finished summarizing the last six seasons of *Friends*, the duchess reached for her teacup. "I do miss television."

"Why did you stay and give up all that you had?" Amelia asked with a furrowed brow.

The duchess's hand stilled as she regarded her for a long moment. "I suppose I followed my heart."

Amelia huffed. "Hearts should not be consulted for making important decisions."

Not appearing offended, the duchess responded, "When you meet your match, you fall in love involuntarily. It's an incomparable, knee-weakening, all-consuming adoration that will not be ignored, no matter how hard you try."

Not satisfied, Amelia pressed forward with her questions. "But you live in a day and age where women are no more than property."

With an indulgent smile, the duchess replied, "The world needs strong women, regardless of the time period."

"I agree with Amelia," Peyton said, accepting a teacup from Aunt Nellie. "Could you imagine being stuck here with no indoor plumbing, air conditioning, or washing machines?" Her mouth closed when she realized the callousness of her words. "I apologize for my harsh remarks, Your Grace."

"Nonsense," the duchess insisted. "You haven't said anything that I didn't think before making my decision. I miss traveling by cars and airplanes. I miss having a competent medical doctor." She lifted her brow at her. "The quacks here always recommend bloodletting and leeches." She shuddered, then took a sip of her tea. "Don't get me started on the incompetence of the dentists."

"Then why?" Amelia asked. "Why would you give up your whole life?"

The duchess's lips twitched in amusement. "You are only asking because you are thinking about staying."

"What?" Peyton exclaimed, turning towards her. "Please say that is not true."

Amelia shook her head adamantly, her curls swishing back and forth. "No, no, no…" Her words trailed off, then she declared too vehemently, "Absolutely not."

"You can deny it all you want, but you love Lord Harrington," the duchess said knowingly, holding up her teacup.

"I… care for him," she hesitated, before adding, "immensely." Her shaky hand went for the teacup before she remembered she hated English tea. "Regardless, this is not my time. I have a wonderful life in 2018."

"I did see you kissing Lord Harrington down by the River Thames today," Peyton stated innocently, taking a sip of her tea.

Amelia bit her lower lip. "He was trying to convince me to stay."

"Did he propose?" Aunt Nellie asked.

"No," she said. "He wants me to stay longer so he can court me properly."

The duchess turned towards Aunt Nellie. "Do you think Lord Harrington is in love with our Amelia?"

"I have no doubt," Aunt Nellie confirmed. "I can see it in his eyes."

Reaching for a biscuit on the tray, Amelia took a moment to enjoy a bite before saying, "No words of love were exchanged. We are merely two people that are physically attracted to one another. That is all."

"That's poppycock, my dear, and you know it as well as I do. Clearly, you two love each other deeply," the duchess stated. "You must understand, nothing in the world is worth having unless you fight for it, and that includes love."

Turning her head, Amelia's eyes took in the rich, red-papered walls. "I have worked my whole life to become a doctor. Why would I give that up?" She rose and put her hands up. "So I could become an aristocrat and live in my husband's shadow for the remainder of my days?"

"I think the question is," the duchess began, "do you gain more than what you give up?"

"I would give up countless years of schooling, an opportunity to help thousands of people, for what?" she said. "For a chance at happiness with Adam."

"I assume that Adam is Lord Harrington's given name?" the duchess asked Peyton, to which she nodded.

Amelia walked over to the window and stared out towards the well-manicured gardens. "It doesn't matter. I must go home. My mother is dying."

"Have you told Lord Harrington the circumstances of your arrival at Twickenham Manor?" Aunt Nellie asked.

She shook her head. "No, he would think I was crazy."

"Mad, dear," the duchess clarified. "In England, you say 'mad'."

Amelia turned around. "I could not bear for Lord Harrington to think I was mad."

"And why is that?" Peyton pressed.

She closed her eyes, mustering up her strength to say her next words. "Because I am in love with him."

"That's no surprise," Peyton mumbled, plopping the rest of the biscuit in her mouth. "But do you love him enough to want to stay?"

"No… yes… maybe?" she stuttered. "Even if we push aside the fact that my mother is dying, I would never be able to work as a doctor again. I would be ostracized for my American citizenship, and no doubt Adam would grow to resent me for what would be considered radical thinking in this era."

Aunt Nellie rose and walked over to her. "Including the duchess, there have been many women that have been in the exact same position as you."

"What did they decide?" she asked.

"Some went back, some stayed, but they all followed what their heart dictated," Aunt Nellie revealed.

Amelia sighed. "And if I make the wrong choice? I could ruin history forever."

Aunt Nellie's face softened with understanding. "Time is a fuzzball. When your string touches another time in the fuzzball, then you are there." She placed her hands on Amelia's shoulders. "Every person has their own thread of time, their own destiny. And you are in control of your own thread."

"Why don't you just tell Lord Harrington the truth and see what he says?" Peyton asked. "If he thinks you are crazy then you'll have your answer."

The duchess picked up her cup and saucer, placing it on the tray. "Just be patient with him. When I finally found the courage to tell the duke about my time travel experience, he withdrew his proposal and didn't speak to me for a week." She smiled. "But he came around. Men in love always do."

"But I'm afraid," Amelia confessed, hugging herself to stop the trembling inside.

"Good," the duchess said. "It means that your heart is longing for Lord Harrington, which renders you emotionally vulnerable."

"How did you become so wise?" Peyton asked the duchess.

"It so happens that I minored in psychology," the duchess revealed, and they all burst into laughter.

Amelia dropped her arms and squared her shoulders. "Why am I acting like a simpering female?" she declared. "I am a modern, confident woman. If Adam does not accept me for who I am, then I will accept that it was not meant to be and go home with no regrets."

"But if you stay," the duchess started, "you will have to start drinking the tea."

Amelia made a gagging face. "It's so gross. How do you stand it?"

"It's an acquired taste," the duchess said with a smile. "Perhaps Aunt Nellie would let me travel to the future, so I could enjoy a delicious Dr. Pepper."

Aunt Nellie laughed. "You are welcome at Twickenham Manor anytime, Your Grace. Now, if you'll excuse me, these two ladies need to prepare for a night at the opera."

Chapter 14

Standing in her bedchamber, Amelia held her mother's coral necklace in her hand. Today, she would tell Adam who she really was. She'd planned to after the opera, but she couldn't find the right words. Over the course of the last three days, Adam would come to call, or she would visit his estate, but still, she could not muster up the courage. It was too easy to get distracted when she didn't necessarily want to bring up such a potentially destructive subject.

Slipping the coral necklace into the pocket of her lavender dress, Amelia muttered, "Today is the day." She would finally know whether Lord Harrington loved her enough to accept the truth. Even if he rejected her utterly, the night of the full moon was only five days away. She could manage until then.

Moving to the window, she pushed back the draperies and saw Adam hopping down from his curricle, striding towards the main door. She gave herself a much-needed pep talk, took a deep breath and walked out to meet him.

As she passed by Peyton's room, Amelia was surprised when her friend ran out into the hall and hugged her.

"Good luck," Peyton expressed. "I'm rooting for you."

"Thank you," she said, attempting to ignore the churning in her stomach.

This was silly. Even though Adam had never admitted he loved her, she was sure that he did. And he would never do anything to hurt her, would he?

Gliding down the stairs, Amelia saw Adam standing in the entry hall, watching her with a smile on his face. She walked up to him, stopped, and returned his smile. "I see that you brought the curricle."

"Are you spying on me?" he teased, offering her his arm.

Placing her left arm into the crook of his elbow, Amelia put her right hand over her stomach. Why did she feel such dread? This did not bode well.

Lord Harrington helped her into the curricle, climbed in, and urged the horses along the path. After Amelia spotted a private location, she placed her hand on his arm and leaned in.

"Would you mind if we took a stroll?"

He gave her a mischievous smile. "Are you attempting to compromise me?"

Amelia laughed. "No. I have something to share with you, and I don't want to be interrupted."

Pulling on the reins, the carriage came to a stop, and he set the brake. As she turned to exit the carriage, Adam touched her elbow.

"Wait for me to assist you," he said.

Nodding, she sat back as he came around the carriage and placed his hands on her waist. He lowered her down, but he did not immediately relinquish his hold. Knowing this might be her last opportunity to kiss him, she wrapped her arms around his neck and pressed her lips to his.

After a moment, he stepped back. "That is my new favorite way to be thanked for assisting you out of a carriage," he teased with a wink.

Instead of offering his arm, he reached for her hand as they strolled through the grassy field. Up ahead, she heard a stream trickling through a grove of trees. She remembered that it was beautifully covered in moss, with little flowers growing on the banks. How she wished this was a walk of leisure rather than a potential walk of doom.

Stopping, Amelia turned to face Adam, attempting to memorize his features. "I have something to tell you, and it won't be easy for you to hear."

"There is nothing that you can tell me that will change the way that I feel about you," Adam assured her, squeezing her gloved hand.

She smiled tentatively. "We shall see about that." Taking a deep breath, she began, "You may have noticed things about me that seemed rather odd…"

"Well, you are American," he teased, interrupting her.

"True, I am American," she started again. "But even in America, I don't fit in during this time."

Cocking his head, Adam released her hand. "I beg your pardon?"

Straightening her spine, she said, "I am a doctor, but I am actually from the future. I belong in the year 2018."

Adam threw his head back and roared with laughter, much to her annoyance. When he calmed down, he smiled down at her. "I haven't laughed that hard in ages."

Placing her hand on the sleeve of his riding coat, Amelia tried a different approach. "Every full moon, Twickenham Manor hosts a ball, and during this time, the magic is activated, and people can travel to another time."

He rubbed a hand over his chin. "What exactly are you saying, Amelia?"

"Twickenham Manor is home to fairie folk, known as fae. It was built to cover the fissure in the earth that allows their magic to seep into our world," she explained, using her hands to emphasize her point. "Aunt Nellie has been the Matron of the Manor for centuries. She gathers the dew on the lawn and plants to create the portraits needed for time travel."

Adam stared at her in disbelief. "Did you forget that I grew up next to Aunt Nellie and Twickenham Manor? It is not possible that she has been living there for centuries."

"Have you seen Aunt Nellie age in all that time?"

With a heavy sigh, Adam asked, "Do you expect me to believe that you have traveled from the future?"

She nodded. "I do."

"I knew that you were too good to be true." Adam turned away from her. "You are mad," he stated.

"No, I am not," she insisted, placing her hand on his sleeve. He shifted his arm, and her hand dropped, shocking her with his rejection. "My mother was named Charlotte, but she went by Lottie, and you met her."

"No!" he shouted. "You cannot invent falsehoods to convince me of something that is not true."

Reaching her hand into the pocket of her dress, she started to pull out the coral necklace, but Adam began walking away. "Wait, Adam!" she shouted. "I have proof."

He stopped and said harshly over his shoulder, "Only my friends have the right to call me by my given name."

She stared at him, shocked. "Are we not friends anymore?"

Adam turned around to face her. "Friends don't lie to each other."

"I am not lying," Amelia stated, stepping closer, holding up the necklace. "You gave this to my mother." She shook it. "You gave it to her as a token of your friendship."

His eyes widened with recognition as he stared at the necklace. "Where did you get this?" he demanded. "Did you steal this from Lottie?"

"No," Amelia declared. "Charlotte Wright is my mother. She went to one of the parties at Twickenham Manor during a full moon. The magic pulled her into your time, but she had to go back home because she was expecting me." She placed the necklace into his hand. "My mother is dying and wanted to see Aunt Nellie one more time, so we traveled to visit Twickenham Manor. My mother, Lottie, sent me to help you. She's been worried about you."

"And how exactly did you travel to this time?"

Her eyes were imploring, willing him to believe her. "I came to your time by stepping through my portrait at Twickenham Manor."

For a moment, Amelia thought she had gotten through to him, but then he huffed. "You are good. Almost believable, in fact." He placed the necklace into his coat pocket. "But you will not take me for a fool, Miss Wright." He turned and started to walk, but away from the curricle rather than towards it.

Standing in the field, she shouted at his retreating frame, "When have I ever lied to you, Lord Harrington? I told you that I did not belong in this time, but you were the one that refused to listen."

Adam stopped and turned back towards her. "Instead of rejecting me outright, you have concocted a story so unfathomable that it belongs in a work of fiction." His words were filled with heartache. "Just go. Go back to being a doctor in America, but don't you dare lie to me."

"I am not lying!" she exclaimed, walking up to him. "I choose you, Adam." She grabbed his lapels. "I will give up being a doctor if it means I will be your wife."

"You forget one thing," Lord Harrington uttered through gritted teeth, stepping out of her reach, "I have not asked."

Amelia reared back as if he had struck her. Her heart plummeted down to her toes, but she wanted to convince him of the truth. "How do you think I knew how to perform that caesarian delivery?"

"You told me that you were a doctor."

"The first female doctor in the United States began her practice in 1849," she informed him. "No medical school in the world accepts females yet."

"What did you hope to gain from your web of deceit?" he asked coldly.

She bit the inside of her lip, attempting to control her emotions. "I came to help you," she pleaded. "You must believe that I did not mean to hurt you. I care about you deeply."

"No, you have demonstrated that you only care about yourself!" Adam shouted, running his hand through his hair. "What am I going to tell Marian?"

"I could talk to her..."

He took a commanding step forward. "You are never allowed to see Marian again," he ordered. "I forbid it."

Despite his thunderous tone, Amelia did not fear him, because she could hear the pain in his voice. "So, this is it?" she asked, her voice rising. "Because once I go home, I will never come back."

Clenching his jaw, Adam replied, "I should have paid attention to my initial impression of you and sent you away."

Hurt by his condescending tone, she tilted her chin stubbornly. "It is your choice to hate me, but I will never look back upon this time without remembering the fondness I felt for you." Tears filled her eyes as she found the strength to express her next words. "I love you, and I always will."

Turning away from him, Amelia began walking back towards Twickenham Manor. "Take the carriage home," Lord Harrington directed.

"I prefer to walk," she replied, not bothering to turn around.

Once she was out of sight, Amelia broke into a run and didn't stop until she dashed through the main door of Twickenham Manor.

"How does this look?" Peyton asked, placing a straw hat with artificial fruit on her head.

Amelia laughed. "I think the large, green grapes really bring out your eyes."

Removing the fruited creation, Peyton put it back on the display stand and pinned her simple straw hat to her head. "This milliner store is fun, but I loved perusing the parasols and umbrellas at Harding Howell & Co.'s."

"Really?" Amelia asked, smiling. "I couldn't tell. We only spent *two hours* there."

"I did offer to get you fitted for a corset at John Arpthorp's establishment, but you didn't think that was necessary," Peyton replied, feigning disapproval.

"I am not a fan of stays, and all these *blasted* layers," Amelia admitted. "I much prefer working in a hospital and wearing only scrubs and…"

"Undergarments," Peyton finished, cutting in. "Amelia, please watch your language. I fear my delicate constitution cannot handle such vulgarity." She smiled, her eyes twinkling with merriment.

Amelia grinned. "I am so glad that you talked me into going shopping in London today."

"It was an entirely selfish thing on my part," Peyton explained as she opened the milliner's door, ringing the bell hanging above the entrance. "Between watching you go riding, reading countless books, and listening to your chatter while embroidering, I was exhausted."

Stepping out onto the pavement, Amelia put her hand in the crook of Peyton's elbow. "It is as I tell my patients, staying idle will do nothing to help ease your sadness." Her other hand became animated as she continued. "Go read a book, learn a new skill, or go work out."

"All excellent points, but those won't mend a broken heart," Peyton admonished, giving her a knowing look.

Watching her kid boots jet out from under her dress as she walked, Amelia attempted to defend her position. "I told Adam the truth, and he did not believe me. So that, as they say, is that."

"No," Peyton drawled. "You told him the truth and confessed your love." She stopped on the pavement. "And he took your heart, ripped it up into little pieces, and stomped on it with his big, black, Hessian boots."

Amelia rolled her eyes. "I took him by surprise, and he did not take it well."

"*That* is the understatement of the year," Peyton teased. "It has been five days, and I have yet to see Lord Harrington crawl over to Twickenham Manor to beg for your forgiveness."

Tugging on her arm, Amelia led them back towards their carriage. "I have no regrets," she insisted. "I spoke from my heart, and Lord Harrington rejected me. It was his choice to do so, and now I can go back to my time without always wondering 'what if'."

"Next time I see Lord High-and-Mighty, I would be happy to kick him in the stomach for you," her friend said. "I have become quite proficient in my jiu-jitsu class. *Hi-yah!*"

"Personally, I would rather see you two in a dance-off," Amelia joked.

"Miss Turner," came a familiar voice from behind. "Wait."

Turning around, they saw Lord Wessex rushing up the pavement towards them. Once he stopped in front of them, he bowed as they curtsied.

Amelia waited for Peyton to say something, but when she didn't speak, she said, "What a pleasant surprise, Lord Wessex. How are you faring today?"

"I am well," Lord Wessex answered, but his eyes were watching Peyton. "How are you faring, Miss Turner?"

Peyton forced a cough into her glove. "I am not feeling well. Please don't come any closer, because I would hate to get you sick."

"Would you be well enough for a carriage ride later this afternoon?" he asked, hopefully.

"No," Peyton stated, shaking her head. "Being outside with this cold would be dreadful, just dreadful."

Amelia hid her smile behind her gloved hand. For some reason, Peyton was pretending to be sick to avoid spending time with Lord Wessex. *Interesting.*

"I see," Lord Wessex replied, his disappointment clearly showing. "Would you save me a dance at the ball tonight, then?"

"I can do that," Peyton assured him. "I will put you down for my first dance of the evening."

"Thank you," Lord Wessex said with a smile. Finally, he shifted his gaze towards Amelia. "I am surprised that Harrington did not accompany you today."

Amelia put on a brave face. "Lord Harrington and I will not be spending any more time together."

Lord Wessex gave her a look of disbelief. "What did he do?" His words were slow and deliberate.

"Nothing. I feel that it is best if I go home tonight as planned," she replied, giving him a weak smile.

"You can't go back to America," he stated firmly. "Adam would be devastated."

Biting the inside of her lip, she attempted to keep her emotions at bay. "I don't think so. We discussed it, and Lord Harrington encouraged me to go home."

Amelia was surprised to see Lord Wessex clenching his jaw, and a muscle below his ear ticked rapidly. "Allow me to assist you ladies to your carriage, and then I will go call on my friend," he informed them.

"You are too kind," Amelia began, "but please don't concern yourself, my lord."

Lord Wessex offered his arms, and they both accepted. As he walked the few steps towards their carriage, he shared, "I am looking forward to the full moon tonight."

Miss Turner sighed. "It will be a night to remember, that is for sure."

Stopping at the carriage, Lord Wessex opened the door and assisted them inside. "Till this evening," he acknowledged softly, his eyes watching Peyton.

Once he closed the door, Lord Wessex stepped back, and the carriage rolled down the cobblestone street. Amelia lifted a brow. "Do you want to explain your fake coughing episode back there?"

Peyton shrugged. "Lord Wessex may have asked permission to court me."

"May have?"

Removing the pins from her straw hat, Peyton placed it on the bench next to her. "Either way, it does not matter," she insisted. "I am not staying here."

"You will hear no argument from me," Amelia said, looking at the window at all the street vendors set up on the pavement.

"Good," Peyton proclaimed, crossing her arms.

"Good."

Neither of them spoke for a long moment, and then Peyton asked, "What would happen if I stayed till the next full moon?"

Amelia's eyes went wide. "You are actually considering it?"

"Perhaps."

"Have you spoken to Aunt Nellie?"

Peyton nodded. "She explained everything to me and said it was my choice."

Smoothing out her dark blue skirt, Amelia took a moment to ponder what her friend was saying. "I suppose the main question is do you love him?"

"I find him handsome, funny, entertaining," Peyton paused, her lips tightening, "but I am not in love with him."

"Fair enough. But could you love him?" she pressed.

"I don't know." Her words were hesitant. "I find him... interesting."

Untying the strings of her bonnet, Amelia replied, "Then why not stay? After all, Aunt Nellie can return you to the same moment as when you left, whether this full moon or the next."

A determined look came to Peyton's eyes. "Good point. I will do it. I will tell Lord Wessex tonight."

"But don't let him officially court you, though; at least until you figure out your feelings," Amelia warned. "Courtship is another term for engagement in the Regency era."

With a wave of her hand, Peyton dismissed her comment. "It will be fun to be courted like a lady, but I have no intention of staying in the nineteenth century."

Amelia smiled at her friend. "You may say that now, but the heart wants what it wants."

"Well, this girl does not want to use a chamber pot for the rest of her life." Peyton giggled. "Or wear these long hat pins that could be used as deadly weapons."

Laughing at her friend's antics, Amelia's eyes drifted back towards the window and admired the rolling green countryside. Flocks of sheep meandered lazily through meadows rich in yellow flowers, stopping to watch the carriage as it passed by.

"I could have been happy here," Amelia admitted softly under her breath. But it was not meant to be. Even though she was returning home, a part of her would always linger behind.

Chapter 15

Sitting atop his horse, Adam stared down from an adjacent hill near Twickenham Manor, knowing that Amelia was leaving tonight. The white estate glowed as the sun began sliding behind the horizon, casting bright rays of light into the sky. His horse pawed at the ground as he rested his forearms on the pommel of his saddle.

Sighing, he leaned back and adjusted his riding gloves. He loved Amelia with a fierceness that he had never known before, but his pride couldn't seem to overlook her obvious flaw. She was mad.

"There you are, Harrington!" Lord Wessex exclaimed as he rode up next to him. "Your stable master was quite vague on which direction you were riding, but I see that I made the correct assumption."

Preferring his own company tonight, Adam growled, "What do you want?"

John grinned. "Nothing but the pleasure of your company, old boy."

"I am in no mood for your tiresome jesting, Wessex. Go away."

"I was in town to be fitted for new shoes, and I ran into Miss Turner and Miss Wright," Wessex began, ignoring his friend's rudeness. "Imagine my surprise when I noticed that you were not escorting Miss Wright. What I find even more peculiar is that she's planning to leave tonight, with your consent."

"You are correct."

"Ah, I see what's going on." Wessex nodded knowingly. "You are trying to find the courage to go and ask Miss Wright to marry you."

Adam adjusted his reins before he turned his horse and urged him home. "No, quite the opposite. I was just saying goodbye."

Wessex followed his lead, and their horses walked side by side. "Why are you letting her go?"

"Leave it alone," Adam warned.

"No, I will not!" his friend exclaimed. "You are making a terrible mistake."

Not wanting to reveal Amelia's shame, Adam chose not to go into the details about his decision. "Trust me, my decision is best... for both of us."

"For the past eight years, you have been a shell of a man," Lord Wessex said firmly. "Then Miss Wright appeared, bringing purpose and joy back into your life."

"I have Marian. She is my purpose in life," he countered.

John shook his head. "Before Amelia arrived, you buried yourself in work, refused to attend any type of social gathering, and barely spent time with your daughter." He stopped his horse. "And now, you have become the man I remember from our youth."

Pulling back on the reins, Adam stopped and turned towards his friend. "It's true that Amelia brought laughter back into our home, but you told me yourself that she was odd."

"Amelia is clever, witty, and beautiful. She would have made a perfect spy for the Americans," John contended.

"Despite being wrong about the spy business, I was not wrong about anything else."

"You wouldn't understand my reasons."

"Then enlighten me."

"Leave it," Adam grunted. "I neither need nor welcome your meddling in the affairs of my heart."

John cast him a frustrated look. "Amelia is your match, in every sense of the word. She completes you, and you won't ever find another woman like her ever again."

"Don't you think I know that?" he exclaimed. "*I love her!*"

"Then don't let her go!"

"It is not that simple," Adam declared, urging his horse forward.

John stared at him. "Why are you not fighting for her?"

"I have my reasons."

"Your reasons are foolhardy."

"I beg your pardon?" he asked. "Besides, aren't you the pot calling the kettle black?"

"This has nothing to do…"

Adam cut him off. "You clearly have feelings for Miss Turner, but isn't she leaving tonight as well?"

"She is," John answered, his jaw clenched tightly. "But I asked her permission to court her."

"And did she agree?"

Sadness swept across John's features, and he realized that he might have gone too far. "Not yet, but I am still holding out hope that she will delay her departure, at least for a while," his friend revealed.

"I'm sorry," Adam mumbled.

"That is the difference between you and me, Adam," John said deliberately. "I will fight until my last breath to try to secure Peyton's love." He huffed. "And you have Amelia's love, but you won't fight to keep it."

Adam kept his gaze straight ahead to avoid seeing the disapproval in his friend's eyes. "It is of little consequence. Amelia is leaving tonight."

John's voice softened. "There is still time. She hasn't left yet."

"It's too late."

John pressed his lips together as his eyes scanned the green countryside. Finally, he turned his horse towards Twickenham Manor. "I agree with you now," John declared. "She will be better off without you, because frankly, you don't deserve her."

Watching Wessex kick his horse into a run, Adam watched him ride towards Twickenham Manor. Soon the sun would disappear below the horizon, and the full moon would transform the sky. He hung his head, knowing that Amelia would be gone before the next sunrise, taking his heart with her.

Throwing open the front door, Adam stormed towards his study, not bothering to acknowledge any of his staff milling around.

"Milord," Mr. Blake said, daring to approach him.

"What?" he growled, hoping his butler would take the hint that he wanted to be left alone.

Instead of retreating, Mr. Blake informed him, "Lady Marian wishes to have a moment of your time before she retires for the evening."

"Send her down," he barked, walking into his study and leaving the door open. He should be pleased that his daughter wanted to say goodnight, but he was hurting.

Suddenly, he stopped as he realized that Marian had been hurting all this time as well. He was fortunate enough to have known Agnes, but Marian had never known her mother. He needed to share more stories of Agnes, for Marian's sake.

He strode over to the drink tray, removed the lid of the decanter and poured himself a double shot of whiskey. Grabbing the glass, he stepped around his desk and sat down on the chair. He threw back his drink and slammed the empty glass down on the desk.

Adam reached down and opened the top drawer, revealing the coral necklace that Amelia had given him. Picking it up, he ran it through his fingers, and the precious memories of Lottie came back to his mind. She had been a true friend. She had appeared when he needed her, but she'd disappeared before he'd had a chance to thank her.

Dressed in a white nightgown, Marian edged into the room and moved towards him. Rising, he placed the necklace on the desk and went to greet his daughter. He opened his arms, and she came running into them, embracing him warmly.

"Goodnight, Father," she said softly. Stepping back, she added, "I hope that Miss Wright will come to play with me tomorrow. I miss her."

He dropped down to his knee and rested his forearm on top. "Miss Wright is going back to America. She won't be visiting again."

Marian puckered her brow. "Did you send her away?"

Ignoring her direct question, he replied, "It was time for her to leave."

Instead of the disappointed reaction he had anticipated, Adam was surprised when her gaze rested over his shoulder. "Why do you have Lottie's necklace, Father?" she asked, pointing at the necklace.

Reeling, he grabbed the necklace and handed it to her. "How did you know that this necklace belonged to Lottie?"

"Because when she visited me, I saw her wearing it," Marian informed him, running her hands along the corals. "She told me that you gave it to her."

"When was this?"

Twisting her lips to the side, she thought for a moment before saying, "About two years ago."

"Where exactly did you see Lottie?"

Marian ducked her head, embarrassed. "I was supposed to be resting, but I stole out of the nursery and climbed the big tree out front." She raised her gaze. "She came to see you, but you weren't home, so she played a game with me."

Lottie had come back to see him! Why had his staff not notified him of her arrival? He cleared his throat. "Where was I?"

"At a meeting," his daughter shrugged, "as always."

"What did she say?"

"She asked if you were home, and I told her no. Then she asked how you were, and I told her that you were sad, and you missed Mummy."

Adam reached out and placed his hand on Marian's little shoulder. "Did she say anything else?"

She nodded eagerly. "She did." She beamed up at him. "Lottie told me that she had to leave, but she was going to try to send her daughter back to help you. She said that we would be friends."

Leaning closer, he asked, "Did she tell you the daughter's name?"

"Yes, her daughter's name is Amelia," she revealed, causing his stomach to clench as if he had been punched. "I know that they are related. Lottie and Amelia look just like each other, don't they?"

How had he not noticed that before? Regardless, this was not making sense. "Dearest, was Lottie as young as Amelia is?"

Marian shook her head. "No, she was much older than Amelia, and she had lots of wrinkles on her face," she said, pulling at her cheeks. "Her eyes were tired, and she didn't look well."

Adam brushed his hand across his face as he tried to make sense of what his daughter was telling him. "Did Lottie tell you when Amelia would come to visit?"

Again, she shook her head. "No. That's why I waited for her at that tree almost every day for the past two years. I knew you needed help, and I wanted you to be happy."

Pulling her into an embrace, Adam whispered, "You have made me happier than I ever thought I could be."

"But Amelia helped you, just like I knew she would," Marian said softly, her eyes downcast. "I was hoping she would stay."

Suddenly, he realized that Amelia's story didn't seem so farfetched. Everything started falling into place. But did he dare to believe that Amelia and Lottie genuinely were time travelers?

For someone who prided himself on always knowing what to do, Adam had to admit he was out of his depth. But this much he knew, if Amelia *were* truly a time traveler, he would go to the end of time to bring her back. *He loved her!* He knew he had a great deal of groveling ahead of him, but he would do it willingly, just for the opportunity to see her again.

Adam leaned in and kissed Marian's forehead. "I've made a muddle of things, and I need to go see if I can convince Amelia to stay with us."

Her eyes lit up with excitement. "Oh, Father! Do you mean it?"

"It might be too late, but I am going to try," he said, rising.

Marian grabbed his hand and started pulling him towards the door. "Blake!" she shouted in the same tone that he usually used. "Prepare my father's horse immediately."

"As you wish, milady," his butler replied with a little bow, his lips twitching in amusement.

Ushering her father into the hall, Marian stood before him and wagged her finger. "Don't forget to use your manners around Miss Wright, and you must control your temper," she ordered. "And lastly, she likes biscuits."

"Blake," she shouted over her shoulder, "could you please bring a basket of biscuits?"

Adam chuckled. "I'm afraid I don't have time for biscuits, but I will keep that in mind next time." He pulled Marian in for a quick embrace. "Wish me luck, darling!"

Sprinting for the door, he headed towards the stable to retrieve his horse, hoping it was not too late.

"I'm coming, Amelia," he mumbled under his breath.

Laura Beers

Chapter 16

For the monthly Twickenham Manor Full Moon Ball, Amelia wore a beautiful, white silk, high-waisted gown with a rectangular bodice and puffy, short sleeves. Marie had parted her long hair down the middle and curled her bangs against her face. The rest of her hair was pinned to the side, except for the ringlets that hung at the nape of her neck.

Leaning back against a column in the ballroom, Amelia watched as the gentlemen led the women towards the dance floor. She blinked rapidly to keep back the tears. She'd been asked to dance repeatedly, but she'd declined their requests. No doubt Aunt Nellie would frown on her behavior, because courtesy demanded that she accept an offer to dance unless she was previously engaged. As much as she wanted to dance, she didn't want to dance with anyone other than Adam. She glanced over at the door for the umpteenth time, hoping that he would appear to at least say goodbye.

Peyton walked up to her holding two glasses of punch. "Would you like something to drink?"

"Yes, please," she replied, accepting the glass.

After Peyton took a sip, she asked, "Has he arrived yet?"

She shook her head. "He isn't coming."

"He's a… a… what was that word you used, Amelia? A ninnyhammer!" Peyton declared, turning towards her. "Lord Harrington doesn't know how incredible you are."

Amelia took a sip of her drink, delaying her response. She was tired of crying over him. "It doesn't matter now. I had a wonderful adventure, and I hope that my limited contribution helped Adam."

Peyton giggled. "You sound more British every day."

"Thank you," she stated, impersonating her best British accent.

"That was awful," Lord Wessex declared from behind her. "Promise me that you will never do that again."

"I promise," Amelia said, smiling.

Lord Wessex offered her a sad smile. "Are you still leaving tonight?"

"I am," she confirmed. "Soon."

"May I ask how you plan to depart?" Lord Wessex asked, hesitantly. "I only ask because the roads are dangerous to travel by night. Between the highwaymen and carriage accidents, you would fare much better if you schedule your departure for the morning."

"You need not worry about that. I have another mode of transportation," she revealed.

That curious furrowing of his brow came back. "Which is?"

Reaching out, Amelia embraced Lord Wessex, much to his surprise. "Thank you for being my friend," she said as she leaned back. "Please take care of Adam for me. He needs a friend."

"No, he needs you," Lord Wessex affirmed, tugging down on his black silk tailcoat.

"Be that as it may, Adam doesn't want me," Amelia said, fighting back the tears. "But please tell him I wish him a lifetime of happiness."

Peyton reached for her glass and handed the two empty glasses to Lord Wessex. "Would you mind finding a place for these while I have a moment of Amelia's time?"

He bowed. "Your wish is my command." He gave her a flirtatious smile and departed.

Peyton embraced her tightly. "Do you really have to go so soon? Why not wait until after the ball? Or better yet, till the next full moon?"

"It is time that I return home and close this chapter in my life," Amelia replied.

"When I get home, I will friend you on all my social media accounts," Peyton said. "Look for my friend requests."

"I will," Amelia agreed, stepping back, "but perhaps you will decide to stay."

"No, I won't," Peyton protested.

Aunt Nellie winked from across the room at Amelia as she left the ballroom.

"It is time," Amelia revealed. "Would you like to come and watch?"

Peyton nodded. "I wonder if someone else will pop in tonight, now that the ley lines are active."

Together, they walked out of the ballroom and up the stairs. Once they arrived on the third floor, Amelia said, "I should change back to the gown I was wearing when I arrived. Can I meet you on the fourth floor?"

Walking into her bedchamber, Marie was waiting for her. She made quick work of changing gowns. "Thank you," she expressed and hugged the maid before leaving the room.

With a feeling of dread that she did not understand, Amelia ascended the final flight of stairs and walked towards the end of the hall. As she entered the room, she saw her mother's portrait, then looked at her own mural, admiring the happiness radiating from her eyes.

"My portrait appears so life-like," she murmured.

"It did turn out well," Aunt Nellie replied, admiring her work. "And Peyton's mural is completed," she paused, looking over at her, "when she is ready."

"I *will* be ready on the next full moon," Peyton declared, a little too forcefully.

"We shall see, dear." Aunt Nellie just smiled at her knowingly. "Now that you both have time traveled, and your portraits are painted, you both can freely time travel through your murals on any full moon."

Peyton walked up to her portrait. "I can travel back and forth in time whenever I want?"

Nellie nodded. "Yes, as long as you are at Twickenham Manor, and the ley lines are open." She turned back towards Amelia. "Are you sure this is what you want?"

"It is," she said. "There is nothing to keep me here."

With an understanding gleam in her eyes, Nellie walked over to her portrait and waved her hand over the length of it. "It can't hurt to put just a dab of magic on the mural." She stepped back, pulling out a little purse and dipping out some dust into her palm. "Amelia, please take your place by your portrait."

Her feet felt like lead as she walked the few steps over to her mural. She knew that this adventure had changed her. She would never be the same again.

Amelia watched Aunt Nellie draw what looked like a clock from the dust in her palm. Her hands came together as she sculpted a magical, glowing ball in the air. The dust swirled around on the inside of the ball. The room danced with a rainbow of colors, and Aunt Nellie started glowing. As she started to raise her hand, Amelia braced herself for the inevitable. She was going home.

Suddenly, the door was thrown open, and she heard Adam shout, "*Stop!*"

Adam could not make sense of what he was seeing. Aunt Nellie was glowing, and a ball of glowing dust was circling around her hand. In a blink of an eye, the bright lights were gone, and he was standing in a room covered with murals on the wall and lighted sconces as if he had imagined the whole thing. Perhaps he was the one going mad.

His eyes immediately saw a large portrait of Lottie, then realized a smaller painting of Amelia hung next to it. "You look just like your mother," he said in wonder, searching for Amelia.

"They do share an uncanny likeness, don't they?" Aunt Nellie agreed as she moved closer to him. "May I ask what you are doing on the fourth floor, Lord Harrington?"

"I have come to beg for Amelia's forgiveness," he said, his eyes never leaving hers. "I was wrong," he hesitated, before adding, "about a great many things."

Miss Turner huffed as she crossed her arms over her chest. "You, my lord, are a daft cow and not worth Amelia's time!"

Amelia let out a soft chuckle at her friend's insult. "That was a good one."

"Thank you," Peyton responded, smiling. "I have been thinking of good insults all day, and I finally was able to put one to good use." The smile faded from her face as she looked back at him and scowled.

Ignoring Miss Turner, Adam stepped in front of Amelia. As much as he desperately wanted to reach out and touch her, he had no right to do so. Instead, he ran his hand through his hair and attempted to recite the speech that he had rehearsed on the ride over.

"Amelia, I am sorry." That was a brilliant start, he thought.

Amelia gave him a wistful smile, and his heart ached at the sight of it, knowing he'd taken the light from her face.

After a moment, she replied, "Thank you for that, Lord Harrington."

"My friends call me Adam, if you don't mind." He gave her a lopsided smile.

"Perhaps you could go into more detail about why you are apologizing?" Peyton asked in an annoyed drawl.

Amelia turned her gaze towards Peyton. "There is no need," she expressed. "I am pleased that we will be parting as friends."

"Wait!" he shouted, his eyes frantic. "That is not what I want."

"Oh, dear," Aunt Nellie mumbled under her breath. "We will give you a moment to discuss…" she frowned, "whatever this is." She walked over to the open door. "Miss Turner?"

Peyton cast him an irritated look as she slowly walked over to join Aunt Nellie.

He frowned as he watched Miss Turner close the door behind her. "I did not realize that Miss Turner was so intense."

"We are friends," Amelia replied, her eyes still on the closed door, "and friends protect each other."

Knowing he had one attempt to set things right between them, Adam turned towards Lottie's portrait and noticed that she was wearing the coral necklace that he had given her. He reached into his pocket and pulled out the necklace.

"I wanted to return this necklace to you," he said, extending it towards her.

She shook her head, sadly. "No, I would prefer that you keep it. That way you will always have something to remember me and my mother by."

This was not going well. "Won't your mother miss it?"

Sighing, Amelia walked to the settee and sat down. "Sadly, I don't think she will even remember it, now. My mother has a progressive disease called Alzheimer's, and she has started to lose all her memories," she explained. "We traveled to England so my mother could say goodbye to Aunt Nellie."

"That must be unbearable for you," he said, sitting next to her. "Are you close to your mother?"

She nodded. "After my dad died, we became especially close, but in a few months, my mother won't even remember who I am."

"Do you hire staff to look after her?" he asked, unsure of how things worked in the future.

"In a way," she replied.

Adam reached for her hand. "No more vague answers," he asserted. "Tell me the truth. I'll try to understand your ways."

She smiled gratefully. "There is a facility, kind of like a hospital, but much cleaner than the ones you have here, that will give her the full-time care that she needs."

"While you work as a doctor?"

"Yes. My schedule is very demanding, and I won't have the time to care for her, even with a full-time nurse to assist during the day," she stated regretfully.

"And you enjoy working as a doctor?"

"I do, immensely."

He watched her, attempting to memorize the details of her face, hoping it wouldn't be the last time he'd see it. "But you were willing to give it all up to stay in England?"

Amelia lowered her gaze to the carpet, but not before he saw several emotions chase across her face. She was trying to be strong, but he didn't want her to hide her feelings from him. He angled his body so he was facing her.

"Amelia," he said, reverently. "I am a fool. I offered you my heart, but at the first test of honor, I betrayed your trust."

"Don't be too hard on yourself. A time-traveling female doctor would have seemed far-fetched to almost anyone."

"I reacted poorly, and I hurt you," he stated. "Please say that I haven't lost you forever with my unpardonable actions."

Amelia smiled, but it was that same blasted wistful smile. "It's better this way."

"Better for whom?" he asked, tightening his hold on her ungloved hand.

"It's best if I go," she remarked, softly. "We live in two vastly contrasting times."

"Yes," he admitted, with a decisive bob of his head, "but I don't want to live without you."

Dropping his hand, Amelia rose and walked towards her mural, stopping in front of it. She spun around. "We would never suit, Adam," she declared. "I was raised in a time where women are treated as equals, I am fiercely independent, and I will never be subservient to any man."

"That's good to know," he replied, rising, "but you are telling me nothing that I didn't already know."

She pursed her lips together. "I think your social etiquette rules are ridiculous, clothing for women is deplorable, and I hate riding side-saddle."

"Duly noted. Is there anything else?" he asked, slowly walking over to Amelia.

"I do not like how children are ignored by their parents, only to be raised by nursemaids and governesses," she continued.

Adam stopped in front of her and placed his hands on her shoulders. "I agree."

Her brow furrowed and a line between her eyes appeared. "You agree with which part?"

"All of it," he replied, slowly trailing his hands down the length of her arms until he held her hands. "I've realized I failed to mention one thing when I asked you to stay before."

"Which was?"

He leaned closer. "I love you, Amelia Wright!"

"You... you do?" she asked, her eyes widening.

He gave her a roguish smile. "I started falling in love with you the moment you stepped into my study for the first time. No one has ever challenged me as you did."

She smiled. "I believe you called me a 'cheeky American spinster'."

"That's true," he confirmed, "but I hope that you will become *my* cheeky American wife." Keeping hold of her hands, he kneeled before her. "I am completely, utterly, deeply in love with you. Will you marry me?"

Adam could see indecision in her eyes, and he was desperately afraid that she would refuse him. "I know that I cannot fully comprehend what I am asking you to give up, but if you will allow me, I will strive to ensure that you will never regret your decision to stay with me," he pressed, hoping that it was enough, hoping that *he* was enough.

Amelia turned her head to look at her mother's mural. "My mother's health is failing…"

"Bring her here," he said, speaking over her.

She winced. "I don't think that is a good idea."

He rose and placed his hand on her cheek. "Your mother saved me. Let me show her the same kindness and love that she bestowed upon me."

"Mum does love England," she murmured, her eyes beginning to sparkle.

"Now that is resolved," he paused, smiling, "please consent to be my wife, and I will spend every day showing you how much I love you."

A tender smile lit her face. "Yes…"

Not wasting another moment, he pressed his mouth to hers, kissing her tenderly, and demonstrating to her without words just how much he truly loved her. Amelia lifted her arms to encircle his neck, molding into his arms.

His lips left hers and slowly started trailing kisses down the length of her neck. "How would you feel about obtaining a special license?" he asked before he started kissing the sensitive skin just beneath her ear, immensely pleased when she trembled in his arms.

"I… think…" she stammered out, breathlessly. "I can't think when you are kissing me like that."

Adam brought his gaze back up, his eyes soaking in her beauty. "I think that's fair, because I seem to lose all rational thought when I touch you." He gave her a devilish smile. "We were discussing a special license."

She leaned in and kissed him, her lips lingering on his. "I have to go convince my mother to travel back, remember?" she said, keeping her mouth close to his.

"No," he stated, shaking his head. "I am not letting you out of my sight."

She chuckled. "I think we should talk to Aunt Nellie, then."

"Good idea," he said, kissing her lips. "But how about in five minutes?"

"Five minutes?"

"I am not ready to let you go," he murmured, bringing his lips to hers and savoring her nearness.

Laura Beers

Chapter 17

Amelia felt as though her heart would burst with happiness. Adam's arms slipped around her waist as he deepened the kiss, and she melted against him. In his arms, she not only felt protected and cherished, but she also felt complete. And his image, touch, and musky scent seemed to be imprinted on her very soul.

"I love you," Adam whispered against her lips.

Her hand threaded through his hair at the base of his neck. "And I love you."

He grimaced. "We didn't make this easy on ourselves, did we?"

"No, we did not." She laughed, resting her head on his shoulder.

The door was pushed open, and Peyton and Aunt Nellie entered the room. "Did you two come to a consensus?" Aunt Nellie asked smiling gently.

Adam stepped to the side but kept an arm around her waist.

"Yes, we have decided to get married," Amelia announced.

"In what time period?" Aunt Nellie inquired.

She smiled at Adam. "I am going to stay here, in this time, because this is where my heart lies."

"But there is no indoor plumbing," Peyton reminded her.

"Indoor plumbing?" Adam whispered next to her ear.

"It is similar to a privy, but I will explain later," Amelia answered. "There will need to be a few adjustments on my part."

Looking back at Amelia's portrait, Adam asked, "May I go with Amelia to the future?"

"You may," Aunt Nellie declared, striding towards the far side of the room. "When you and Amelia first met, it was clear that you two were destined for each other." She picked up a portrait that had been leaning against the wall and took a moment to admire it. "The magic even hinted to me that you might want to journey through time to visit Lottie again."

Peyton looked at Amelia and mouthed, "Hinted?"

Hiding a growing smile, Amelia shrugged one shoulder.

Aunt Nellie walked back to them and turned the portrait over, revealing a perfect likeness of Adam. "It turned out well, if you ask me."

"It did," he replied, studying his portrait carefully, "and I can time travel through this painting?"

Aunt Nellie smiled fondly. "You can and will," she answered confidently as she leaned the portrait against the wall and stepped back.

Reaching for his hand, Amelia did want to make sure he understood what he was getting into. "Just so you know, everyone has some pain or discomfort associated with time travel. I had ringing in my ears."

"I was nauseous," Peyton spoke up.

"Both are common effects, but they tend to wear off within a brief period of time," Aunt Nellie informed him. "Now, shall we?"

In preparation, Adam placed his arm around her shoulder, tucking her against him. "Are you ready, my love?"

Hearing those words from his lips made her soul rejoice. "I am."

Aunt Nellie removed the bag, pouring dust into her hand and started drawing what looked like a clock from the dust in her palm. Her hands came together as she sculpted a magical, glowing ball in the air. When the space around Aunt Nellie started glowing, Amelia felt Adam tightening his grip on her shoulder, as if attempting to protect her.

"Here you go!" Aunt Nellie shouted, holding the magic like a pulsing star. Then she clapped her hands together.

Suddenly, everything went white, and she felt like she was being blasted from a cannon. Then, Amelia fell onto something soft, and she heard a deep grunt. She took a moment to adjust her eyes and hoped that the ringing in her ears would subside soon.

"Welcome back," Aunt Nellie declared. "And you brought a gentleman friend along."

Amelia heard soft steps come closer. "Are you all right, Lord Harrington?" Aunt Nellie's voice asked from above her. "I am pleased to see you have arrived in one piece."

His voice came from beneath her. "I am… alive," Adam sputtered, coughing.

Realizing that she had, in fact, landed on Adam, she pushed herself off him. "Sorry, Adam."

Blinking his eyes, Adam grunted a bit breathlessly, "You can always count on me to be there when you fall, my darling." He shifted his gaze towards Aunt Nellie, and his eyes widened in amazement. "How is it possible that you look younger now than you did in the past?"

Aunt Nellie smiled faintly, but it didn't extend to her eyes. "That is a most pleasing way to be greeted." She lifted her arm and looked at the watch on her wrist. "Unfortunately, Amelia, you have arrived almost one hour after you departed."

"Is that a problem?" she asked, making her second attempt to stand.

Aunt Nellie assisted her to a standing position. "Your mother collapsed after you left. She is with the doctor now."

Forcing herself to focus, she asked, "Is she in the same room as before?"

"She is," Aunt Nellie confirmed.

Amelia glanced at the floor where Adam was still sprawled out. She couldn't leave him, but she knew his effects were only temporary.

Aunt Nellie must have seen her indecision because she stated, "Just go. We will look after Adam."

Bounding along the hallway towards her mother's room, Amelia opened the door and saw a middle-aged man in a tweed sport coat with elbow patches. He stood with an air of seriousness over her mother's bed. He was listening to Lottie's heart with a stethoscope, frowning.

Taking a deep breath, Amelia pushed aside her fear and slipped into her familiar doctor mode, asking, "What can you tell me about my mother's condition?"

The doctor straightened up to assess this younger, vibrant version of his patient. "You must be her daughter, Dr. Wright?"

"Yes, I am," she confirmed, striding closer to the bed to shake his proffered hand.

The doctor leaned back from the bed as he explained, "Your mother collapsed, and her heartbeat is growing weaker. I am afraid there is not much time."

"May I?" she asked, pointing at the stethoscope.

Accepting it, she listened to her mother's heart. Reaching for her mother's clammy hand, she saw the skin was a mottled bluish-purple, which was a sure sign that death was near.

Mustering up strength, she replied, "I concur with your prognosis, doctor."

The gray-haired gentleman offered her a look of compassion over the top of his glasses, the same look she had given her own patients on occasion. "We could transfer her to a hospital. That might buy her some time."

Amelia shook her head. "No, that would just prolong the inevitable."

When she handed back his stethoscope, he said, "Well, if I can be of any further assistance, please give me a call."

"Thank you, doctor," she managed to say, but her eyes were fixed on her mum.

Once she heard the door latch, Amelia sat down in the chair next to the bed and tears began streaming down her face. She thought she'd have more time with her mother. A loud sob passed through her lips, and she felt her heart shatter. Then she felt a warm and comforting hand lay securely on her shoulder. Turning around, she saw Adam standing beside her, taking in her mother's waning form with compassion and wonder.

"It's truly Lottie," he said softly.

"It is. But she is dying."

Adam stepped forward and reached for Lottie's hand. In response, her eyes blinked open. "Lord Harrington," she said in a weak voice. "Adam, my dear friend, is that you?"

"It is, Lottie," he replied, his voice catching with emotion. "I have traveled a very great distance to see you."

"I never had a chance to say goodbye," Lottie asserted, her voice regaining some strength. "But as my Amelia grew older, I knew she could help you."

A tear ran down Adam's cheek, but he did not attempt to wipe it away. "You saved me, dear lady. Not once, but twice." He looked back at her daughter. "Thank you for sending Amelia to me."

Her mother lifted her other hand, encouraging Amelia to reach for it. "I knew... I had to get Amelia to travel to your time... because I knew you belonged togeth..." Her voice trailed off as she started coughing. "I wanted you to have each other... when I am gone."

"Mum," Amelia breathed out. "You should be more focused on yourself right now."

Lottie shook her head. "No... my time is short. But I wanted to make sure you were taken care of, my dear... before I passed on."

"You need not worry about Amelia," Adam vowed in hushed tones, his gaze full of tenderness. "I will ensure she will never want for anything, especially love."

"Thank you, Adam," her mother replied, her voice barely a whisper.

Adam leaned forward and brushed a piece of hair off Lottie's face. "No, Lottie darling, it is I that should be thanking you. All that I have, and all that I will become, will be because of your friendship. You rescued me that day in the river, allowing me the chance to live, and to love again."

Her mother's eyes drifted closed, but a smile came to her lips. "I knew you two... would suit."

Releasing her hand, Adam grabbed another chair and positioned it next to Amelia's. For the next few hours, he held her as they watched her mother grow weaker. She felt stronger with him by her side, buoyed by his silent support providing her with great comfort.

With love and gratitude in her heart for her mother, Amelia smiled at the thought that her mother had intended for them to fall in love. Mum hadn't given up on her, but she had been fighting for Amelia all along.

Staring out of the blasted window of Twickenham Manor for the thousandth time, Adam grew more and more irritated by Amelia's delay. "She said she would be back within the hour," he grumbled under his breath.

Glancing over at the floor clock, he saw that she was two hours late. Why was her meeting with her attorney taking so long?

Aunt Nellie looked up from embroidering a handkerchief. "Perhaps you would like to practice your embroidery, Adam." She grinned. "After all, isn't this what you will expect Amelia to be doing all day when you are at your meetings?"

He chuckled. "I daresay Amelia does not have the patience to embroider."

"You sell your betrothed short," Aunt Nellie replied. "After all, she is an excellent surgeon."

"I have witnessed that firsthand."

Aunt Nellie lowered her embroidery to her lap. "I do have some reservations about Amelia returning to your time."

Adam sat down on an upholstered armchair next to her. "Pray tell, what are they?"

Placing the handkerchief onto a side table, Aunt Nellie faced him and said, "In our day, Amelia is a highly competent, highly successful doctor from a top medical university. I am concerned that you will attempt to suppress her intellect, and she will have no choice but to return back to her time… without you."

Fear gripped his heart. "You don't think she would abandon us, do you?"

"It depends," Aunt Nellie expressed. "Will you treat her as a true partner, and a woman that you cherish and love?" She lifted her brow. "Or do you intend to marry her with the intention of her succumbing to the role of a nineteenth-century woman?"

Adam looked down at the Persian carpet, taking a moment to compile his thoughts. "That is a ticklish question, Aunt Nellie," he replied, bringing his eyes up to look at the twinkling lights in the wall sconces. "I have every intention of marrying Amelia and treasuring her for the remarkable woman that she is. I will give her the freedom to make her own decisions, and I will never expect her to change who she is for me." He sighed. "However, the ton are a fickle lot, and there will be times when she will need to conform to the social norms of our day."

Reaching over, Aunt Nellie patted him on the leg. "There is a saying in our time; 'Happy wife, happy life'." She smiled.

"I think that is wise counsel." His eyes roamed the drawing room, and he could not believe the changes evident in this room alone. "I will miss these brilliant lights," he said as he looked at the twinkling lights on the wall.

"Ah, yes, you mean the light bulb," Aunt Nellie muttered, following his gaze. "Lovely invention, but that wasn't until 1879."

"It's fascinating," he said, walking closer to the wall sconces and putting his hand close to the light bulb. "Much more practical than candles."

"I apologize that I have asked you to remain close to Twickenham Manor, but I feel that it is best for you not to experience too many of the vastly different changes in culture between our times," Aunt Nellie explained.

"It is hard not to see the differences, especially since I see cars out my window," he shared, turning back to face Aunt Nellie. "Don't worry, Amelia has told me about cars, planes, and even air conditioning."

"Air conditioning," she murmured. "Another wonderful invention."

Adam ran a hand through his hair. "Tomorrow is the full moon, and I worry that Amelia will not be ready to depart."

"Poor Amelia has been quite busy. She had to travel back to America to bury her mother, settle her mother's estate, and officially withdraw from her residency program at Harvard," Aunt Nellie said.

"I would have liked to have traveled with her, but Amelia informed me that I do not have a passport," he recalled. "Which, apparently, is important when you travel here."

"It is," she confirmed, her eyes perusing his garments. "In addition, you would stick out like a sore thumb with your clothing style."

Looking down at his buff trousers, paisley waistcoat, and a white linen shirt, he asked, "What is wrong with my style of dress?"

"Nothing," Aunt Nellie raised her hand to hide her dimpled smile, "if you are an English gentleman from the early nineteenth century."

"It is a good thing that you have a room full of Regency-era dress clothes," he stated, tugging down on his waistcoat. "Although, the quality of the fabric is much finer in my day."

Amelia's voice broke into their conversation. "I, for one, would not change a thing about your appearance," she declared, sauntering into the room and placing her purse on a side table. This gave him time to admire her black trousers, loose, flowery top, and high-heeled shoes. With a smile, she moved towards him and didn't stop until she kissed him on the lips.

Placing his hands on her hips, Adam lowered his head, very gently resting his forehead against hers. He stayed there and breathed her in. "I've missed you."

"I've missed you as well," she said, her eyes full of merriment. "I have good news."

He pulled her closer. "Good news? Does that mean you are ready to go back to my time and marry me?"

She leaned forward and kissed him. "That is already a given."

"Then what is your good news?"

Aunt Nellie spoke up, "Perhaps you two would like to take a stroll around Twickenham Manor on one of our many lovely paths?"

"That is an excellent idea," Amelia replied, reaching for his right hand. As they left the room, she grabbed her purse.

Adam could feel the excitement build in each one of Amelia's steps as they walked out the main door, and he couldn't wait to discover the reason. Once they reached a bench that faced the River Thames, he made sure she was seated comfortably before he claimed the seat next to her.

"I was dreadfully bored as I waited for you," he shared. "I even considered embroidering."

"Dear me," Amelia mocked, touching her fingertips to the base of her throat in feigned shock. "You poor, poor man."

He laughed as he had not laughed in a long time. Only Amelia could make him feel like he would burst with happiness at any moment. "Life with you will most definitely not be dull."

"I am sorry I have been so busy these past few weeks, but it could not be helped."

"You never need to apologize to me."

"But I do," she said softly. "You have been so incredibly patient and supportive of me, and I want to thank you from the bottom of my heart."

Bringing his hand up to rest on her cheek, Adam expressed, "My only regret is that I could not have been there to help you bury your mother."

A wistful look came into her eyes. "That was hard."

"I am here now," he stated, his eyes imploring hers. "Never again will you have to face another obstacle alone."

"For that, my dear Lord Harrington, I am most grateful." Leaning forward, she kissed him, an aching slow kiss that left him with an intense longing for more.

Adam reluctantly broke the kiss. "Tomorrow cannot come soon enough. I will secure a special license, and we will be wed as quickly as possible, my lady."

"I think that's a grand idea, my lord." She grinned. "I have more good news as well." She reached into her purse and pulled out a large, black velvet bag. "My parents were quite well-off, and I wanted to bring my inheritance back with me.

Luckily for us, Aunt Nellie recommended a way for that to be possible."

He stilled her hand. "That is unnecessary. I have amassed a fortune of my own, and you will want for nothing."

She gave him an understanding smile before she opened the bag, revealing precious gems of all sizes and shapes. "This is only a portion of my inheritance."

"This is only a portion?" He started to exclaim before he lowered his voice. "What you are holding is worth hundreds of thousands of pounds in 1813."

"I know," Amelia said. "I wanted to use this money to establish a hospital... and run it myself." She held her breath, waiting for his response.

"I think it is a brilliant idea," he declared.

"You do?"

"I do," he insisted. "We will need to find some forward-thinking doctors to work in the hospital, because I have no doubt that you will play an active role."

"Thank you for understanding how much this means to me." Her words were filled with emotion as she tied the string on the bag.

Adam tucked a lock of brown hair behind her ear. "I fell in love with a female time-traveling doctor, so I logically concluded that your life as a doctor was far from over."

She leaned down and placed the bag back into her purse as she shared, "The other portion of my inheritance has been set aside in an account for when we travel back to this time..."

He cut her off, suddenly defensive. "Why would we need to travel back to the twenty-first century? For what purpose?"

"Well, you don't have to travel back with me. I just assumed..."

Adam stood up and placed his hands on top of his head, pacing. Amelia was already planning on traveling back to her era and leaving him behind.

Unexpectedly, Amelia's hands wrapped around his waist, and she laid her head against his back. "The only reason I would want to leave you is that I want to have our babies in a modern hospital."

He stilled. "Babies?" he asked, turning around in her arms.

"I had assumed... uh," she hesitated, "that you wanted more children." She lowered her gaze. "I know that we hadn't talked about it, but..."

He cut her off by pressing his mouth to hers. After they parted, he said, "I am sorry, my love. I was worried that you would grow to regret your decision to stay with me. Then, when you mentioned time traveling, I just panicked..."

Pressing her finger against his lips, Amelia stilled his words. "With every breath, every heartbeat, I love you more." Her eyes glistened with tears. "You will always be enough."

"Even more than indoor plumbing?" he teased. "Because I agree with Miss Turner's sentiments. It *is* brilliant."

She laughed. "Even more than indoor plumbing."

Tightening his hold around her waist, he expressed, "Marian will be pleased to have you as a mother."

"To think I had given up on ever finding love." Her amber-flecked eyes were deep wells of affection as she watched him. "Then you came along, my unexpected gentleman, and I have never known such joy."

"I have one rule," he whispered against her lips.

"Anything."

"Wherever you go, I go," he said. "If you choose to travel through time, I will be at your side."

"I wouldn't have it any other way," Amelia agreed, sealing their words with a kiss.

Epilogue

A highly-amused Adam leaned against the wall in Amelia's managerial office, hiding a bemused smile behind his hand. His very pregnant wife placed her hands on her polished mahogany desk and leaned forward in her imposing leather armchair.

"Would you care to repeat that, Dr. Wilcox?"

Calmly, Dr. Wilcox removed his spectacles and wiped them off with a handkerchief. "I was merely pointing out that because of your advanced age," he placed his spectacles back onto his rather long, pointed nose, "you may have complications during childbirth."

Amelia's eyes narrowed. "I am only twenty-eight."

"Yes, which is well past the ideal age for childbirth. You must be grateful that Lord Harrington was willing to overlook your age when he chose you to be his countess." Dr. Wilcox gave Adam a confused look. "Didn't your doctor inform Lady Harrington about how age affects childbirth?"

Rising with difficulty, Amelia's flashing eyes never left the doctor's face. "Please come here so I may hit you," she invited in a deliberate tone.

"I b-beg your pardon, madam?" Dr. Wilcox stammered.

Amelia placed a hand to her back and waddled precariously around the desk. "I said 'Come here so I may hit you', you incompetent quack!"

Dr. Wilcox's expression was most decidedly annoyed. "Lady Harrington, even though your body is going through changes, you must consider your reputation."

Pushing off the wall, Adam stepped to intercept his wife before she made good on her promise to punch the doctor. He easily caught up to his wife and placed an arm around her shoulder, halting her forward progression.

"Dearest, it is not seemly to use fisticuffs in a facility that treats the ill and injured."

The doctor humphed. "I was told that 'the Countess of Harrington Hospital' was forward thinking and using new techniques to help the sick. Unfortunately, I was not informed that the matron was mad!"

Having had enough of this pompous doctor's attitude, Adam proclaimed, "You are dismissed, doctor, and your application will not be considered."

"B-b-ut, Lord Harrington..."

"No buts," Adam declared, cutting him off with a decisive wave of his hand. "My wife runs this hospital, and you have made the grave mistake of insulting her."

Amelia leaned towards the seated doctor with her hands on her hips, nearly toppling over, and asserted, "Most abominably."

Adam chuckled. "My wife was not pleased that you said that she was 'of advanced age'."

The doctor took off his glasses and attempted to ignore the unbalanced woman looming over him. "Lord Harrington, if I may..."

"Good *day*," Adam proclaimed, suddenly stern. He kept his gaze firmly on the doctor until the self-righteous man stormed out.

Amelia moved to leave the support of his arm as she said, "Thank you, dear husband."

Adam tightened his hold and brought his other arm around her expansive waist, engulfing her in his arms. "I believe I deserve a reward for saving you from that pompous and arrogant doctor."

Smiling up at him, Amelia's hands slid around his neck. "What would you like?"

"A kiss," he murmured before his lips pressed against hers. Breaking the kiss, he kept his arms around her, relishing her swollen body. "Are you ready to go home and rest before we leave for Twickenham Manor?"

"I most assuredly am," she replied, rubbing her large, protruding belly in a circular pattern. "Our little boy will be coming any day now." The next Harrington gave a mighty stretch, which caused Amelia to gasp and clench her side.

Adam shook his head in amazement. "I still find it miraculous that a metal tool could swipe over your stomach and allow us to see inside of you. Furthermore, I still can't grasp how this magical tool can tell the gender of the babe."

Laughing, Amelia said, "I find your descriptions adorable. Once we are in the Lindo Wing at St. Mary's hospital, I will tell you the name of every instrument being used."

"Do I really have to wear those chinos, polo shirt, and loafers again?" he asked, shuddering. "Those articles of clothing make me feel as though I am going out in public positively undressed!"

Amelia smiled. "Only if you want to see the birth of our child."

"Fair enough, my lady," he mumbled.

Arching an eyebrow, his wife remarked, "It is not like I am asking you to wear stays, a petticoat, or any of the layers that I am required to wear on a daily basis."

"And I thank you for that," he joked. "Although, I must admit that I am grateful for your modern medicine to help with our son's birth."

"Careful, my lord," she murmured. "It almost sounds like you aren't opposed to our holidays in 2018."

Brushing a wisp of hair from her glowing face, Adam said, "I wouldn't call visiting your doctor a holiday."

"I would." She smiled. "I get to take off these ridiculous clothes…"

"Which I always welcome."

She laughed as he hoped she would. "What I meant was that I get to wear jeans and ride in a cab."

"Those metal cars are unusually prompt, but I prefer a carriage," Adam informed her.

A young female nurse ran into the room, her eyes appearing frantic. "Lady Harrington," she proclaimed, breathless. "We need you in the operating room. A child was run over by a carriage and was just brought in."

In the blink of an eye, Amelia's face grew purposeful, and she went into what she described as her 'doctor mode'. "Thank you, Sarah. Have you alerted Dr. Williams?"

"We have, and he will be in shortly," Sarah informed her.

Waddling over to her desk, Amelia picked up her apron and kissed her husband's cheek. "Please fetch me in a few hours.

I want to eat supper as a family before we go to the Full Moon Ball at Twickenham Manor."

"Yes, my love," he said fondly as he watched his wife leave the room. Adam grabbed his top hat off the coat rack and walked out of his Harrington hospital, knowing his heart was truly full. He allowed Amelia to follow her destiny, and in return, he had a wife who was loved by the entire county for her medical insight and her kind heart. While he was at his meetings, his wife dutifully ran her hospital and saw to Marian's lessons, which now included a broad range of subjects.

In their home, they freely expressed themselves, laughed without restraint, and every night, they assembled to eat together as a family. Never had he known such joy in his life, and it had all started because he fell in love with a cheeky, American, time-traveling doctor.

The End

Did you like this book?
Please consider leaving a review.

Don't forget to check out the other books in the Twickenham Time Travel Series:

— P.S. I Love You by Jo Noelle
— Love's Past by Laura D. Bastian
— Against the Magic by Donna K. Weaver
— Mistletoe Mayhem by Jo Noelle
— Love Match by Jo Noelle
— An Unexpected Gentleman by Laura Beers
— With the Magic by Donna K. Weaver
— Dating the Duke by Jen Geigle Johnson
— There's Always Tomorrow by Laura D. Bastian
— Enchanted Heart by Jaclyn Hardy

About the Author

Laura Beers spent most of her childhood with a nose stuck in a book, dreaming of becoming an author. She attended Brigham Young University, eventually earning a Bachelor of Science degree in Construction Management.

Many years later, and with loving encouragement from her family, Laura decided to start writing again. Besides being a full-time homemaker to her three kids, she loves waterskiing, hiking, and drinking Dr. Pepper. Currently, Laura Beers resides in South Carolina.

You can reach her at authorlaurabeers@gmail.com

Made in United States
North Haven, CT
28 May 2022

19615163R00124